CALEB

WINCHESTER BROTHERS BOOK 1

KATHI S. BARTON

World Castle Publishing, LLC
Pensacola, Florida
Copyright © Kathi S. Barton 2017
Paperback ISBN: 9781629896212
eBook ISBN: 9781629896229
First Edition World Castle Publishing, LLC, February 6, 2017
http://www.worldcastlepublishing.com
Licensing Notes
Cover: Karen Fuller
Editor: Maxine Bringenberg

PROLOGUE

"Dag nabbit boy, what is wrong with you? Do you have sawdust in that noggin of yours?" Caleb said he wasn't sure. "I'd be thinking you'd better be getting sure if you wanna live through this here thing. Your momma, she's going to be having herself a kitten if I don't miss my bet."

He looked over at the truck, or what was left of it. Caleb wanted to tell his dad that it wasn't his fault, that he'd done nothing wrong, only he was sure that he'd still be in trouble. Caleb had been driving and he had hit the tree.

"I'll pay for the damages." His dad said he darn tooting was. "And I'll make sure that the tree is all right. I don't know how I'll make that happen, but I will. Mr. Wheedle likes this tree, and I would feel bad if it died."

The tow truck arrived about ten minutes later, and Caleb saw his mom get out of it almost before it was completely stopped. She asked him if he was all right, then she hugged him. Caleb waited for her to make sure he wasn't bleeding profusely, then stood straighter when she glared.

"Where were you going in an all-out hurry?" He told her he wasn't speeding. She looked at the truck, which was on the dolly now, then at him. "You want to tell me why the truck, the only vehicle that we have, is all mangled up like those towels you left on the floor this morning?"

"I wasn't driving fast, but the wolf that ran out in front of me seemed to be...I think it was hurt." He looked over at his dad, then at the ground again as he continued. "A wolf came out of nowhere. I wasn't going to hit it, but it seemed to just jump in front of me. Like it was trying to kill itself. I swerved to miss it and lost control. I'm not blaming the wolf, because I was the one driving, but I didn't want to hurt the wolf. But like I told Dad, I'll pay for all the damages and work on the truck until it's running again."

Neither of his parents said anything and Caleb looked up. They were looking at each other, and he felt his wolf run over his skin. There was something going on and he had no idea why, but he thought they believed him about the wolf.

"This wolf, you ever seen it before? I mean, around the house?" He said that he'd not. "Can you tell me if you thought it was a shifter or just a regular old wolf? And I need you to be sure, so if you don't know, then say it."

"It was bigger than a regular wolf. Of that I'm sure. But as for whether or not it's a shifter, no, I don't know." His mom nodded and looked at his dad again. "May I know what's going on?"

"You know old Mr. Cartwright?" He asked if she meant his old math teacher. "Yes, that'll be him. His mate died a few days ago. She was poorly for a while now and she just passed on. Mr. Cartwright, he was with her a good long time. Said he didn't think he could live without her."

"So he was trying to kill himself?" Caleb's mom said nothing, but he could see the hurt on her face. "Mom, I didn't hurt him. I missed him by a mile. He...I like that old man. I hurt that he does."

"I know you do, son. So do I. To lose a mate…you know how that would make me feel should I lose your father." She hugged him again. "But I need for you to do me a favor. A big one. And before you say something, yes, it is a lie, but it's a good lie. Don't tell anyone what happened here today. The pack will frown on him trying this."

"All right." He looked at the truck, then back at his parents. "I'll still take care of this. I swear to you that I will. And I'll make sure that I keep a better lookout for Mr. Cartwright, too."

"You do that, Caleb. You go on ahead and do that for him." Caleb and his dad made their way to the tow truck. "You know why we don't want you to say anything? I mean, the real reason?"

"No sir." He watched his dad help Mom into the tow truck. She didn't need it; Caleb knew that, but he loved watching his parents together. They loved each other the best, he thought. Always thinking of the other one no matter what was going on.

"Mr. Cartwright loved his mate. I know that you understand that part of it, but he had nobody but her. They don't have themselves any children or anybody else to call their own. If he were to die like this, by suicide, the pack wouldn't bury him in a proper way. They'd just let his body rot in the field where he crawled to and let him just be more alone. On account'a that, he'd not be next to his mate in the cemetery. Understand?"

"Yes, sir. He's a good man who's suffered a great loss." His dad said that was it. "I'll go on over and see him later. I won't mention what happened, just see if he wants to go fishing or something. Keep him company."

"You're a good boy, Caleb. All you boys are. I'm right

proud of you." Caleb felt his face heat up with embarrassment. "Now, you go on home. I'll work something out with the driver here. We'll muddle through this. I swear it."

Caleb knew that his family ran right on the edge of poverty, like a lot of families around here. But unlike most of them, his family had food on the table nightly and they had power and heat. His dad worked hard every day to make sure of that. And he and his younger brothers, all of them, did everything they could to help too. This wrecking of the truck, however, was going to hurt them for some time.

Instead of going home, he found himself standing in front of the Cartwright home. Mr. Cartwright was sitting on the front porch, rocking in his chair like he was going someplace. And he was crying. Caleb coughed, then cleared his throat to make sure to give the older man a little bit of time to collect himself.

"What are you doing here? Don't you have enough to do around that farm of yours that you should be here bothering me?" Caleb nodded and told him he had plenty to do, but wanted to ask him something. "Whatever it is, you don't have any business asking me. Go on home."

"Would you like to go fishing with me? I sure could use a nice little break today. And I know you have that nice stream that goes behind your house." Mr. Cartwright stopped rocking and asked him why he needed a break. "I had myself an accident earlier. My mom, she's not mad at me. More glad that I'm all right, but I'd like to make it up to her by bringing home some meat for dinner."

"And that means what to me? Are you telling things that aren't true, boy? You do that and I'll come after your entire family." Caleb asked him what he meant by that. "What did you tell your parents about wrecking the truck?"

Caleb looked at the ground again. He'd not said a thing about the truck, or wrecking for that matter. Mr. Cartwright would only know that if he'd been there. His parents were right in what they had thought.

"I just needed to take a little break, that's all. I thought.... Well, I guess you have more important things to do than to spend a lazy hour with a kid." He nodded at him, his heart hurting for what the man was going through. "I'll see you around, Mr. Cartwright."

"Now hold on there a minute. I never said I'd not go." He stood up and Caleb tried not to notice how his face was a little scuffed up and that he was walking slower than usual. "You and me, we'll go fishing today, but I don't want you to make a habit of just showing up here. You need to be working on your math more than you need to be fishing with an old man."

Mr. Cartwright got them both some gear and even packed them up a nice basket of food to share. There was sweet tea to go with it, too. As they made their way down to the stream, Mr. Cartwright told him about how he had a good recipe for trout, and that he had some stored apples still from last year.

The two of them caught nine trout and two catfish. As he was helping the man gather up their papers from the food and the gear, Mr. Cartwright asked him if he'd take the entire catch with him to his house.

"I already told my mom what I caught. She said that there was so much, you should come join us." He hadn't talked to his mom, but knew that if Mr. Cartwright would agree then he would. "She even baked a nice peach cobbler today. I was smelling it this morning. I'm betting there might be some homemade ice cream too."

In the end, Caleb was able to convince Mr. Cartwright to

join them, and his dad said he'd dig out the old churn, that ice cream sure did sound good. The cobbler was the only thing he'd not lied to the man about. It was, after all, what he'd asked for as his special dessert for his birthday. Caleb Kelley Winchester was seventeen today.

As he walked the man back to his house, they didn't say much. He was stuffed as he'd ever been, and eating with the man beside him had made for a great gift, one he'd not expected to get. When he was up on his porch, Caleb turned to go home when Mr. Cartwright said his name. Caleb turned back to see him standing there with a sad look on his face.

"My wife is gone. I know you know that, but I hurt with it. Worse than I ever dreamed I'd be, and that was a lot." Caleb said he was sorry. "I'm sure you know it was me that caused you that accident. And.... Well, I'm sorrier than I can tell you that you missed me."

"I'm not. Had you died out there, I would have killed a great man on my birthday. I don't think that would have settled well for me, do you?" He shook his head. "Mr. Cartwright, if you don't mind, I'd very much like to hang out with you sometimes. I'm sorry that you hurt so much, and there isn't anything I can do to fix it, but I really enjoyed today. And the meat was an added bonus. You're a good man, and I liked today."

"I did too. It's the first enjoyment I've had in a while." Caleb nodded. "And if you want to come by here and see me, I'll not be sorry about that either. You're a good boy, Caleb. I hope you know that."

"I hope so. My mom will be really disappointed in me if I'm not." He laughed with Caleb. "I'll come by tomorrow, sir. And we'll see about fixing that leaky roof that you were telling me about. All right?"

"Yes, I'd like that. I might have a few other chores around here that you can help me with too, if you'll allow me to pay you for them." He said that wasn't necessary, but he'd like the company. "I would as well. I'll see you tomorrow then."

Caleb returned home with a lighter step. He knew that things were going to be tighter now. His dad had told him that the truck towing alone cost nearly fifty dollars, more than he knew his parents had. He was going to go see Shelton in the morning to see if he could work off a bit of that a week. Caleb was going to hold to his promise of paying for the damage.

~~~

Arnold sat on his rocker and felt better than he had in a while…since his wife had taken her last breath, as a matter of fact. He wiped at the tears that fell, thinking that he just hurt to think about her too much.

"I failed you, my darling. Failed to come to you today." He looked in the direction that the young Caleb had taken. "I should have been a little more selective of who I ran in front of, I guess. An older driver, he wouldn't have been that quick to swerve to miss me. But I got me a friend out of this mess I put me in. A few of them, I think. And the trout was almost as good as you made me on occasion."

Rocking more, he thought of the Winchester family and how meager their table had been tonight. He wondered what they might have eaten had they not brought the fish to them. But whatever might have been on their table, he was sure that they would have enjoyed it and felt blessed by it. He rocked a little harder.

"They got themselves nothing to get around in because of me. I did that to them. I heard that boy telling his daddy that he'd make it right. And I have a feeling that he will too. No matter the cost to his time." Arnold paused in his rocking to think of what he could do to make it up to them. "That old truck out back, I think they'll be able to use it, don't you?"

He thought of other things that he had that he no longer had any use for. He'd give it to them, to make up for what they'd lost. But he'd have to be sly about it. Arnold would not take their pride from them. And he knew for as much as they didn't have, their pride was a thing they valued a great deal.

Pulling his phone toward him, he called Shelton Bloom. When he answered his phone on the forth ring, Arnold had to laugh. He was sounding like a man who might need a break himself.

"Shelton, it's Arnold Cartwright here. I wanted to talk to you about the Winchester truck that you brought there today." Shelton told him it wasn't worth fixing even if they had the money. Arnold had already figured that was what he'd say. "You got anything there that they can use up? I'll pay you for it. Not top dollar, but I'll pay you for it. That boy, Caleb, he's going to be running me around, and I need him to have something to use."

"There are two old beaters in the back that run all right. But I don't know, Mr. Cartwright. You might need something better than that. I'd surely hate to think of the two of you broken down on the side of the road. How about I let him take that car that Masterson never paid for? It's a beauty and runs like it's in its second childhood." Shelton understood what he was doing, even if Arnold was a little nervous about it. "I think it'll hold you both, and his family, should they need to be on an outing together. What do you think? It won't cost you a thing either. Mr. Masterson said I could have it for working on it."

By the time he hung up the phone, he'd planned to have the towing paid by him and his old truck looked at to make sure it was running well. There wasn't any reason why he couldn't drive himself around, but to have that boy helping him might be worth it. As he settled into his chair again, Arnold spoke to his lovely wife.

"I might not be joining you just yet, my love. This family, I have a feeling that they need me as much as I do them. And I have a powerful need to help them out." He nodded into the darkness, thinking of how much more alive he felt because a boy hadn't killed him like he'd wanted. "You just hang on tight and I'll be there soon enough. I need to be helpful to them and in return.... Well, I think they're going to be more helpful to me than I ever thought."

Over the next few weeks, not only did he get his leaky roof fixed by Caleb, but he also got his lawn mowed, his bushes trimmed, and he even got the steps to his barn repaired. Not only did Caleb help him, but the rest of them, including that mom of his, lent him a hand or two.

He had berries in his freezer, and a few little pies he could eat when he wanted. His pants were patched up, and there wasn't a single button missing off any of his shirts. His wife, Thelma, she'd been sick for a time, and those things had gone by the wayside. It was nice having the house all aired out and the sheets on his bed to be fresh. It was like they'd adopted him, and he was liking it.

Caleb was in his yard, mowing the last of the grass, when he realized how much more he could help this boy. College. He needed this boy — hell, all them boys — to go to college. Arnold also knew that the Winchesters would be lucky to send one to college, not to mention six of them. So he set about, in his own little way, making that happen as well.

And he sat down to dinner with them every night too. Sometimes there was meat, most nights not. But Arnold didn't mind. He was with good people, and that made up for his belly being just a little upset with him for not having a hunk of meat in it. He decided to help them out with that as well. Arnold was having fun. Helping these people was fun.

"I need me a person to work for me full time." Caleb's father asked him what he needed and that he'd find him someone. "No, I'm talking about you, Kelley. I need you to come work for me full time."

"Mr. Cartwright, you're a very nice man. And I have to tell you, you couldn't have helped us out any better than giving us that vehicle to get around in. Mary said it's a real treat for her to go shopping and not have to load it all in the back end of that old truck of ours. And don't think I don't know that you've made a few other things happen for us too. I'm appreciative of it, I swear to you. But you don't have to go making up work for me. I'm glad to help you out." Arnold started to speak, but Kelley cut him off before he could. "Caleb is learning a lot from you. How to be a better man, and to know that not everything he does needs to have a payment in the end in the form of money. I thank you for that too. But like I said, you've done about enough."

"No, I've not, Kelley. Without you—without that boy there—I'd be dead now. We both know it." Kelley nodded and Arnold nodded before continuing. "That day that I hurt him—and I know that it did—but that day he gave me something I'd not had in a long while, since my wife took ill. He gave me purpose. And this job that I have for you, it's not a made up one. I do need you. I have...I don't have anyone else."

"You know that I'll surely be glad to help you. You're a good man." Arnold thanked him. "What is it you need help with? I'm not too smart, but I'll give it my best shot."

Arnold had no doubt whatsoever that he would too. Yes, sir, he was going to have the time of his life with this family.

CHAPTER 1

Caleb heard his office phone ring, but he was right in the middle of putting together an ad and couldn't stop just yet. He wanted to get his project done before he left for the weekend. He was going home, and nothing was going to mar his time with his family. He looked up when Selma said his name.

"It's your father. He said that it's important." He nodded and bent over the file again. "Caleb, he sounds really upset."

He snatched the phone up and pressed the button for the line she told him his dad was on. As soon as he connected, he heard his dad crying. Not just crying, but sobbing. He asked him three times what was wrong before he answered him.

"He's gone. Arnold, he passed in his sleep and he's gone." Caleb sat down, not even realizing that he had stood and grabbed his coat when he first heard his dad. "The pack master came over to tell me in person that he'd been found in his bed. He said he'd passed peaceful like, and that he looked like he'd just gone and closed his eyes and that's it."

"Oh, Dad, I'm so sorry." His dad cried harder, and Caleb felt his own eyes fill with tears. "He was a great man. All he's talked about is going to be with his wife. I think he's at peace now. And I'll miss him so much."

"They're going to bury him this weekend. I thought with

you coming home and all, we'd go as a family." Caleb said he'd be there. "Good. Good. Your brothers are gonna be here too. I called you first, but I know that they're coming."

"Yes. I'm leaving tonight and I'll be there pretty late, but I'm coming. Is Mom okay? I know that she's been over there a lot lately." His dad said that she had and she was taking it awfully hard too. "I'll be home soon, Dad. If you need anything or the pack does, give me a call."

Caleb wanted to leave then but knew that he had to finish the project first. Mr. Cartwright was gone; it was hard to focus on the art when that was all that kept circling around in his head. That man had come to mean a great deal to him over the years. He'd been a grandfather to him when he'd had none.

Caleb knew that the elderly man was getting up there in age. Even as a teenager, he thought the man was old. But he never acted like it, not after that first week Caleb had started to help him out around the house and farm he owned. Mr. Cartwright told him once that he thought he was born old. But to think of him not being there when he came home, it was too much to bear.

It took him an hour longer than he had hoped it would to finish up. Caleb was shutting down his computer and locking up his desk when his boss, Mr. Lancaster, came into his office and sat down. Caleb tensed up, not wanting to hear whatever the man had to say.

Mr. Lancaster—David, he insisted on everyone calling him—was a dick. And Caleb disliked him more than he did anyone he knew. The man was a terrible boss, lazy, and he took advantage of Caleb and the rest of the people that worked for him a great deal.

"I heard that you were still here. I was hoping I could get you to do a few things for me over the weekend. You don't have a family or anything that needs you, so I know that I can depend on you to do it. Right, old buddy?" Caleb said that he couldn't, he had plans. "I'm sorry to hear that. I guess I'll have to find someone that can be there for me all the time."

Caleb would normally have said he'd do the job, whatever it was. But lately, just over the last six months or so, he was getting to the point where he didn't want to do anything but what was necessary. It wasn't like him to be like that, but he didn't like his job and didn't care all that much for the people that he worked for. Especially David Lancaster.

He was still sitting in the chair across from him when Caleb stood to get his coat. The file that he'd been working on was locked up, the work on it had been emailed to the prospective client, and everything in his desk was cleared away for Monday when he returned. Caleb was just picking up his keys when David leaned back in the chair and let out a long breath.

"I really need for you to do this for me, Caleb. It will go a long way in getting you that raise you wanted. I can get others to do it for me, but I'd rather it was you. The rest of the group aren't like you. They have families to go home to, and we all know what you think of that institution." Caleb asked him what that was supposed to mean. "You're never getting married. We both know that. It's why you can work so late and on holidays when the others, the family men, have things to do. Besides, this project, it's right up your alley."

"I told you, I have plans this weekend." As far as Caleb knew, David had no information on him other than that he worked for him. He'd never taken the time to get to know him in the ten years he'd worked there, and he doubted the man cared for anyone but himself. "If you're ready to go now, Mr. Lancaster, I can lock up behind you."

"Perhaps you didn't understand what I was saying. I need you to do this for me, and you're going to. So, I'm not going to go until I tell you what it is I need. You'll do it, Winchester, you know you will. I have no idea why you're playing hardball with me, but you need this job more than I need you working here." He laughed and patted the seat beside him. "Come on back here and I'll give you the details on the project, then you can go. It's really not that hard. Anyone can do it."

"Then why don't you get someone else to do it?" Caleb never talked back to people, especially his boss. But he was hurting with the death of his friend, and didn't care right now who hurt right along with him. "I really need to get going. I have a long drive ahead of me. So, if you're ready to leave, I can—"

"The project has to do with the new dogfood account we just landed. Thanks to you, the client is very happy to be working for us. Anyway, the client wants it to be snazzy. I have no idea why he thinks that his customers, who are dogs by the way, will care if the advertising is snazzy or not, but he seems to think we can give it to him." He patted the seat again. "Caleb, how will you take notes if you don't have a seat? The mock ups for the new labels are in an email that I sent to you. Also, there are some choices words that he wants to have in the—"

"I'm terribly sorry, Mr. Lancaster, but I have to go." He shook his head. "You can lock up if you wouldn't mind. I'll work on whatever you want on Monday when I return."

"You're not going anywhere and we both know it. You come in here, have a seat, and I'll tell you what I want." The hard tone had him pausing at the door to go back and do what he was told. He nearly did what the man said, but he spoke again. "You're stupid if you think that if you walk away from this I won't fire you. Come on now, have a seat."

"I quit." He felt better with those two words out there than he had in a while. "Yes. I quit. I've been working here for a long time and you treat me like shit. I'm really sorry, Mr. Lancaster, but I just can't work for you any longer."

He was nearly to the elevator to take him out of the building when he realized what he'd done. Caleb had just quit his job. But instead of feeling like he had fucked up, he felt relieved, his body and mind settled. This was the only thing he could have done and lived with himself, he realized. It was well past time to be out of there.

As soon as he got off the elevator, he had to pause. It wasn't like him to be rash about things like this, less so with his income. But he needed this, more than he thought he would. Smiling, he made his way to the security desk and hoped there wouldn't be any trouble.

He handed his badge to the security officer at the front desk and let him not only look through his briefcase, but wand him as well. Billy smiled at him when he handed him his briefcase as well as his jacket and keys back.

"Got a message I'm to detain you. For theft." Caleb said he'd not taken anything. "I can see that. And even if you did, I don't really care. I think you did the right thing, getting out while you can. You need to branch out, get set up with your own company."

"Thank you." Billy told him to get moving, that Lancaster was on his way down too. He was stopped once more when he was opening the door. Billy handed him a small thumb drive.

"It's the cam of you quitting and how it went down. All with time, dates, and audio. In a couple of days, I'll be sending you the ride down to here and my report on what

I found when you left. Don't let it get in the wrong hands." He thanked him and told him he'd hold onto it. "See that you do. Good luck, Caleb. You're going to need it. Or maybe not. You're a good man."

He hoped his parents thought that too. Caleb wasn't sure what he was to do now as he got on the bus to take him to his tiny apartment. He wanted to go back and beg for his job again. To call his mom and ask her if he'd made the biggest mistake of his life. But he stayed where he was. Because he knew, deep inside, that it was all there had been left for him to do and live with himself.

He'd packed his bags before leaving for work this morning in anticipation of going home. Caleb added a clean suit and tie, as well as his dress shoes. Then for fun he added the loudly colored shirt that Mr. Cartwright had gotten him for his birthday this summer. The man would have had a good laugh about it had he still been around. Caleb decided that he was going to wear it under his suit coat.

The drive home was quiet. Caleb didn't listen to music that much, preferring his own thoughts as company than the strum of music. Christmas music was all right, as well as nature sounds, but the holiday was still a little too far away and the sounds of nature made him homesick. Running water and the sound of a thunderstorm on a summer night were just what he'd hear at home. He thought of Mr. Cartwright and their conversation on his last visit.

"You ever thought of going out on your own? Being your own boss?" Caleb thought he was kidding and laughed. "I've seen your work. You're a mite better than I think most people give you credit for. Surely that boss of yours knows the gem he has in you."

"I doubt it. Mr. Lancaster thinks I'm a moron." Mr.

Cartwright asked him if he thought he was. "No. Thanks to you, I have a good education and a job. Not a great job, and certainly one that doesn't pay all that well, but I can send money home to Mom and Dad every month, and I have a roof over my head. I don't think that's too much to ask for in life, do you?"

"You still paying off the truck? Boy, that was nearly fifteen years ago. I think you paid for it and then some. Besides, I thought I told you I took care of that." Caleb said that he knew that, but he knew his parents needed the extra. "I guess they do. Those brothers of yours, they sure do eat. I was over for dinner the other night and I swear, I thought for sure your momma had cooked a whole cow. Not a bit of leftovers either. And she can bake a pie like nobody else I know."

"My dad said that farming doesn't pay like it used to. And I think he's sort of worn out from it anyway. But last year, Mom and Dad were able to go on that nice vacation with a little to spend, thanks to us sending them money. I think Dad felt guilty about it, but he said it was worth that just to see Mom having so much fun." Mr. Cartwright said that he'd heard about their trip too. "I miss them, being in the city all the time. But I have my freedom too."

"Freedom is wonderful. And lonely." Caleb asked him if he was lonely. "I am. I miss my wife. She was the best thing that ever happened to me, not counting you and your family. You still thinking you don't wanna marry? Sad thinking that."

"I'd love to settle down and have a wife and a couple of kids. But I have nothing to offer a woman. You know that more than anyone." Mr. Cartwright pointed out that he had a heart, a good one as a matter of fact. "Perhaps, but that won't pay the bills, nor will it put children that we might have in college."

23

"Possibly. But it would mean a happiness that you'll never find again." He told him he was happy. "No. You've settled. You're no happier than I am a young man. And we both know that I've managed to outlive rocks in the ground hereabouts."

Those words had stung. Not that they were the truth, but they hurt him none the less. As he pulled into his parents' driveway and saw all the lights on in the house, he knew that this would do for him. Happiness was his family.

~~~

David was not a happy man. It was Monday and there was no sign of Caleb. David now had to call up his client and tell them that the project would be delayed. For how long he had no idea, but at least long enough for him to convince Caleb that he needed this job and promise him things that he would never follow through on. The nerve of the stinking little shit thinking that he could just walk away without notice. The knock at his door made him sit up straighter in his chair. Bidding the person on the other side welcome, he told the man to have a seat.

"I have that file that you asked for. However, it doesn't show anything you want it to." David said that it didn't show anything just yet. "I'm not sure what you mean. Mr. Winchester left his office without incident after telling you that he quit. The elevator ride down was uneventful, and he turned in his badge, even letting me go through his things and wand him, as you told me to do."

"You'll see. I'll say that he hit me, both up here and down in the front lobby. And you'll back me up, Billy, or you'll be out of work as well." Billy Wacom sat there for several seconds, his face a study in concentration. "I have a buddy that can make this look just like I said it would."

"But that's not right. He didn't do anything like that."

David asked him why he even cared. "Because Caleb isn't like that. He worked hard for you and did what you wanted, even losing time with his family."

"So? I gave him ample opportunity to do as I wanted. All he had to do was take a few hours and finish a project that I wanted done. I think that was the very least he could have done, under the circumstances." Billy asked what the circumstances were. "I pay him to work for me. And when he quit...well, I might have to let some people go if this client pulls out. Things have been a little tight around here of late."

Billy said nothing, but David knew that he was thinking hard. The man, sadly, knew a great deal about why the company was having money issues. Billy's father worked as a security guard at one of the casinos in town, and had helped him be escorted out a few times. David, like most men he knew, was a sore loser.

"Caleb isn't going to come back here, I don't think." He asked him why he'd think that. "He seemed happy when he left here. I mean, like I've not seen him in a long while, happy. No, I don't think, even if you try to blackmail him with a doctored recording of the day he left, he's ever going to come back here to work."

"You just do your job and I'll do mine. By the end of the week, not only will Caleb be working for me again, but he'll do it with a cut in pay. I can't have my best worker going out on his own and thinking that's going to be all right with me." Billy nodded and stood up. "If anyone asks you, you have no idea what was on this recording."

"I won't lie. You can fire me if you want, but I won't lie. Not about this or anything else that goes on here." David stood up too and asked him if he was threatening him. "No, I won't call it that, but I do know a lot about the goings on here, and you should know it. There are cameras around here that I don't think you know about. If you did, you'd be a bit more discreet on some of the things you do to people."

After the man left, David sat there fuming. The nerve of people lately, thinking they could treat him this way. As he put the thumb drive in his computer he thought of what Billy had said. Were there cameras that he didn't know about?

When his dad had this place, he had thought it a good idea to have security cameras put in everywhere. Not the bathrooms…that was the only place that David knew for sure that his dad hadn't had them installed. David would have to do something about that soon. But for now, he wanted to watch the sap Winchester deny him what he wanted. His phone ringing had him pause the thing just as Caleb had walked out the door of his office.

"I was wondering when I could see some mockups of the advertising on the dog food. It's been nearly three weeks and nothing." David tried to make his voice sound professional, but all he wanted to do was hit the man on the other end of the phone. Alexander Dorsey was becoming a pain in his ass. "You told me that you'd have your best man working on it day and night. Yet here I sit with nothing. Are you even trying, Lancaster, or are you twiddling your thumbs while I wait on you? I want you to know that I won't wait much longer. The time frame we gave you is nearly up. You'll be in breach of contract if you go past it."

David wished every day that he'd given Caleb the information on the ad campaign when he'd gotten it, which was weeks before he'd entered his office that night. But things had gotten in the way…a good deal on some coke that he'd gotten with the payment of the ad. Then there had been the house that he'd found himself in and not a clue how he'd gotten there. David had also wrecked his car. There was always something to distract him.

"I do have him working on it, even as we speak. He did have one mockup done, but it just wasn't his best work so I had him redo it. He'll do this one better, I assure you. I think he's sort of punishing me because I thought he wasn't putting his heart into it." Dorsey asked to have those sent to him. "I'm afraid that's not possible. He...I trashed them. I can't have shoddy work going out when I know we can do better."

"Trashed them? Without letting me be the judge of my own ad? I've seen this man's work, and frankly, he's the only reason that we went with your company, Lancaster. This Winchester person doing my work...well, as I said, it's the only reason we had you working for us." He laughed a little. "And you had better remember that, Lancaster. You work for me, not the other way around. Get me something today or I'll find someone else to do it for me. I'm not playing around here. I need this ad for my new product. Today."

The phone disconnecting had David steaming. He'd actually hung up on him, like he was nothing more than a minion...less than that, he was nothing. And to think that he believed that Caleb was the only one that could do what he did was just ludicrous. He picked up the notes from Dorsey and made his way out to the work area.

He stood up on the desk closest to him and whistled. It was puny and not at all what he wanted, but it had the desired effect. The people working in the big open room all turned to look at him. David held up the paperwork that he had brought with him. He'd get this done, by God, or someone's head would roll. He might even kick it a few times while he was at it, damn it.

"There is a thousand-dollar bonus for anyone that can get

this finished by lunch." He glanced at the clock, seeing that it was nearly that now. "All right, by close of business today. A thousand dollars."

No one moved. After a couple of minutes, two of the ten working went back to their computers. He repeated his offer, thinking that they might not have heard him, but still no response. One man stood up and David made his way to him.

"Can I have that in writing?" David asked him what he meant. "The bonus. If I get this done, you'll pay me, I guess, but I'd like it in writing."

"You don't trust me? Christ man, you work for me." He said nothing, but he didn't take the offered paperwork either. "What if I just told you to do this without the bonus? You'd damn well like it better with it, wouldn't you?"

"I don't even know what that means, but if you make me do it, I'm not sure I can get it done when you want it. I can see right there on the paperwork that you've had it nearly a month. That's a long time without having anyone do it. What about Caleb? Where is he?" Good question, but he didn't say that to the idiot in front of him. "Oh, that's right, he quit. Smart man, Caleb. If you want me to work on it and try to get it done by tonight, I'm going to have to have it in writing that you're going to actually pay me the bonus. You've pulled this before on us."

"When? You know what, never mind. I will not be blackmailed like this. You'll do this project and you'll have it done by the end of the day, or you're fired." The man took the paperwork, but David had a feeling that he wasn't going to do any more than a half assed job at it. "Did you hear me? I said you'll have it done or you're finished here. And don't think I'm going to forget that you tried to blackmail me. That shit just isn't going to fly with me."

"I heard you. But you should consider this; if I go, so does most of your workforce." He walked away without explaining. David was just pissed enough to ask him what the fuck he was talking about. The man turned to the group in general. "If I don't get this done as I've been ordered to do, I'm done. Is there anyone here willing to work for a man that would threaten you like that? If not, then will you walk with me?"

Every one of them stood up and nodded. These fuckers were going to piss him off if they did that. But instead of threatening them too, he stomped off to his office. He wasn't sure, but he thought he heard laughter as he did. His father wouldn't have had to put up with this shit. As soon as he entered his office, however, he nearly turned and left. The man himself, his dear father, was sitting at his desk as if he owned it. Well, he did, but there was no reason for him to be here at all.

"Got you some trouble, don't you, son?" He didn't bother answering him, but sat down in the chair that he wished his father was in. There were things on his desk, a lot of things, that he'd just as soon not have to explain. David could see the line of coke he'd put out before the phone call earlier. "Imagine my surprise when Alexander Dorsey called me at home to tell me that you're fucking with his ads. Please tell me you're not. I won't believe you, but you can tell me that. And where is Caleb? I came here to talk to him about something."

"Gone. He quit. After knocking me around." His dad cocked a brow at him. "Well, he did. Not any bruises that you can see, but he got violent with me and I had to call in security. If he hadn't walked out, I would have had him fired. I don't need to be fearful about my job. So, he was escorted out by security."

"You mean Billy? I already spoke to him. When I asked him where Caleb was, he told me that he quit on Friday and that you wanted him to lie about some recordings. He won't, just so you know. And I wouldn't allow it, even though you did threaten him with termination." Christ, his head was going to explode. Did anyone do anything he wanted anymore? "What are you going to do, David, run everyone off? If that's your plan, I think you should just step away now. I worked hard to make this company what it was the day I retired, and in the few short years that you've been in charge, there has been a huge turnover, not to mention you've lost your best worker. That is not the way to run a business. Unless, of course, it's your plan to run it into the ground."

"I'm not leaving. You retired. What the fuck are you doing here, anyway? Checking up on me? I don't need it." His dad asked him if he was sure. "Of course I'm sure. Damn it, Dad, I'm doing just fine."

His dad stood up. "Sure you are. And in a couple of weeks, less I'm betting, Caleb Winchester is going to open his own advertising firm and we're going to shut down. Because as talented as the man is, you're just as stupid."

David was going to make his father and everyone else that didn't believe him eat their words. As soon as his dad was out of his office, David sat down at his desk and pulled out his rolled up one dollar bill. Up until recently it had been a hundred. Times sure were changing, he thought.

It wasn't often that he had to get a hit this soon after having one for breakfast, but he'd had a very hard morning so far. Taking a nice long snort, he leaned back in his chair and thought of nothing, just the way he liked it.

CHAPTER 2

Caleb walked out on his parents' deck and sat down. There were a lot of people in the house, all of them coming to their home to celebrate the life that had been Arnold's. He'd lived more in the last few years than most people did their whole life, some said. And Caleb knew that was true. He'd been so full of life when he'd been home last.

"May I join you?" He nodded to Daniel Hatfield, the pack leader of Arnold and their pack. After he was settled in the seat, he smiled at him. "He loved you like a son, I think. If he could have, I think Arnold would have joined your family. He never said anything like that, but I believe in the last few years, he spent more time with you and your family than he did with anybody else. It's a good thing, don't get me wrong. Your family gave him a reason to breathe in and out every day."

"He told me once that he liked being a wolf. That it afforded him things in life that he wouldn't have had as a human. I think he had a good handle on things." Daniel nodded. "You know that he liked you a great deal as well, don't you?"

"I do. Arnold wasn't a man to take friendships lightly. And I'm pretty sure that he would have told me straight up had he found me lacking." They both laughed; that would have been exactly what he would have done. "I have to tell you something. You're not going to be happy about it, but I must all the same. He left you something in his will."

"No. He told me that he wouldn't do that. He was to leave it for the pack." Daniel told him he'd left them the land that surrounded his home to roam. "Good. I think the pack needs more ground to call our own. He was a very generous man while alive, and that's all I ever need from him."

"Be that as it may, he still left you part of his estate." Caleb said nothing, but Daniel didn't seem to mind. "Two weeks ago, he called me to his home and had me sign off on a few things. Mostly it was what he wanted done with the land. How we couldn't sell it or develop it. I was fine with that. He also made stipulations on your parents' land. He took care of them as well."

"He didn't have to do that. My parents are doing all right." Daniel said that they were. "I don't think I want to know whatever it is you're working up to. I mean, I loved the old man, with all my heart. He kept me out of a lot of trouble when I was younger, and he's been a great friend to me over the years. My whole family."

"He did. And I know that you saved his life as well." Caleb waited. He had no idea if Daniel knew everything or not, but he'd never tell. "When I was called here, he told me how you'd wrecked your parents' only means of transportation that day trying not to hit him when you were a mere pup. He also told me that had you hit him and killed him, he'd left me a note to know that he'd done it to himself. His heart was shattered by the death of his wife. But you...I think that in some way, you saved his life that day, not just by not hitting him, but you breathed life into the old man."

"I'm sure I don't know what you're talking about." Daniel

nodded, but the smile grew wider. "He was sad, I know that. Much like I am now. I wished, more and more over the years, that I had gotten to know Mary. From his stories about her, she was a pistol."

"She was when we were children, too. Mary was my much older sister." Caleb said that he was sorry, he'd not known. "No one did. We thought—and I believe that Arnold was correct in thinking—that had anyone known that was gunning to take over the pack, they would have stopped at nothing to get to him and Mary. She was the best thing that ever happened to me. And when she married Arnold, my life seemed to be about perfect. Arnold and Mary were the perfect couple."

Daniel sat there for a little while longer, neither of them feeling the need to fill the silence. He thought of something that Arnold had said to him on more than one occasion... there was no need to be emptying your head all the time. Quiet reflection was better than babbling.

The crowds started to dwindle down after about an hour. Caleb and his brothers, all five of them, had started the process of cleaning up when Robert Butler, Arnold's attorney, asked to speak to them for a bit. He said that it was important that he got it done today.

His dad said that it was fine by him if he didn't mind them taking time to clean up too. Robert said it was all right by him, but he thought they might want to pay attention to him. They all ended up in the living room, along with Daniel.

"This is the reading of the will of Arnold Latin Cartwright. Everyone mentioned within this will is present and accounted for. There is—"

"Now hold on a darn minute here. You should be doing this at your office. I mean, we got no cause to be listening in on that private stuff. You should be.... Unless it's for some witnessing, but I don't think we should be hearing what that poor man left for everyone." His dad looked around the room at them all. "We were close, that man and us, but I don't think that we need to be here for this."

"He left you some things." His dad shook his head. "He did. All of you. He loved you all very much, and his generosity in the friendship that he shared with you is all he had left. He wanted to make sure that you were as cared for as he was."

"I don't know what to think about this. He was a good man. He didn't have to go and do anything like this. Maybe he had a family somewhere out there that might benefit from it. But if he did, then they're gonna hear from me. To leave that poor gentleman all alone like this." He had no one, Robert told his dad. A quick look at Daniel and Caleb kept his mouth shut when he shook his head. "He had us."

"Yes he did. And I'm to tell you that this is in stone, what is written here. Arnold said that I was to make sure that you all knew that these were his wishes, and that you cannot go and change them. He was a feisty man, all the way to the end." They all nodded. Caleb could almost see the old man telling the attorney how to keep them all in line. After getting the legal things out of the way, Robert started on what he called the meat of the will. "For the pack, he leaves the seven thousand acres around the house, minus fifty acres that go with the house, to roam as you please."

Caleb was shocked. He knew that there was a bit of land around the house, but not nearly that much. After he was given the deed to the place and the rules that would govern it, Daniel left them. He said that he had to let the pack know what was going on. And that he knew the rest of the will.

"To Kelley and Sara Winchester, I leave the holdings in

three companies that I own. You have been the dearest friends to me over the years, and I wanted you to have something that could keep you in matches in the winter and tomatoes in the summer. You are the best people I have ever had the pleasure of meeting." His dad laughed, and so did his mom. Robert laughed too. "He told me how you were forever running out of matches, and that Sara could make the best tomato dip he'd ever eaten."

"I'm going to sorely miss him, I am." Dad blew his nose as he held Mom. Caleb loved his parents, more than he thought possible, in that moment. To hurt so badly for a man twice their age. "Go on now. Tell them boys what they got so we can go out and have a nice howling."

"All right. To Gabriel Winchester I leave my account at the bank." Robert looked at his brother as he continued. "The bank will have all the necessary paperwork you need to sign it over. Per his statement here, he wants you to use it for your practice. He said for you to get your ass in gear and open your own place."

Gabe was working on becoming the best country doctor there ever was. He might do it too, with the extra money. No matter what it was, he knew that Gabe would use it for just what Arnold had said.

"To Owen, I give you my watches. All of them are to do with as you please, and I think you should sell them. But the one that I carried when we were boating, that one you should keep." Owen nodded and smiled. "I'll make sure that you can get into the safety deposit box in the morning, if that is all right with you?"

"Yes. That's fine. Watches. I love it. He would have one in his pocket that was never wound, because when you were on a boat, time meant nothing, he told me." Owen laughed again.

"Mr. Cartwright could have spent his life out on the lake, and it surprised me to no end because of him being an elderly man and all."

"He told me that it made him feel like he could conquer the world. You and he, he told me that he enjoyed his time out there with you. You were never one to jabber." Owen nodded, sadness deep in his eyes. "To Xander. I should tell you something before I tell you, Xander. He thought you were the funniest man alive. He would tell me some of your.... Well, he'd tell me your stories, and he would just laugh his butt off. For you, he left the ability to write."

"Write? You mean a book? I told him that I didn't have time for that. I have to work." Xander stood up and began to pace. "He told me that I needed to get this story that I have in my head down. How on earth...? He left me the ability to write, but I don't know a lick about it."

"There is a publisher that is willing to take you on. Arnold also lined you up with an editor, as well as someone to help you out with research. There is more too, but I can give it all to you when we're done here, if you don't mind?" Xander sat, but he didn't look happy. Or perhaps he was just embarrassed. "For Tyler, I leave you my homes. It's not much, he goes on to tell you, but there is money enough for you to do improvements as you see fit. You also have some acreage that goes along with it."

"His home?" Tyler looked at Caleb, then back at Robert. "I thought he'd leave that to Caleb if anyone. I mean, he spent the most time with him. Not that I don't appreciate it, but that seems more of a gift for him."

"Arnold left him other things. But for you, he left the homes he owned." Tyler was clearly confused, but everyone was happy for him, including Caleb. Robert cleared his throat.

"To Dominic I leave my lovely wife's trust. He wanted you to be able to finish your education without having to work yourself to death. Nor put a drain on your parents. There is also a car with it, for you to travel back and forth to college. He said that you're a smart man, and that he thought you should pursue your dream of teaching."

Everyone looked at him. Caleb stood up, his heart breaking for the man who would no longer be there for him when he needed him. He thought of all the conversations that he'd had with the man, the dreams that he'd shared, and mostly, the insight that he'd given him on life.

"He gave me more than enough while he was living. More than I think I deserved at times. He gave me his friendship and his heart." Robert said that he'd given Arnold his as well. "He made it very easy to love him. And respect him. I don't care if there is something in that will that he wants me to have, it's never going to bring him back."

"No. It won't. But he has plans for you as well. He gave you downtown." He asked him what he meant by that. "Arnold was...I noticed that not one of you asked about the value on what he gave you. He told me that you wouldn't. Even laid a bet down, and you know how much he hated to part with cash. But he told me, right there in my office, that this family wouldn't care that he left them anything. He even told me that Kelley here would be upset that he'd included him in his will. But you, Caleb, he wanted great things to come to you. He left you buildings in the downtown area that he has owned for more years than you have been alive."

"How much?" They all turned to his mom when she asked the quiet questions. "How much did he leave us? I know that sounds horrible, but now that you bring it up, I'd like to know."

37

"For you and your husband, you're now worth just over six million dollars at today's market value. Gabe? Everything told, there is about fifty million in all his accounts. The watches that he gave Owen? Fair market, I'd say they were worth just about that much. One of them is valued at just over two million alone. Xander's gift is a little trickier. With the offices that he opened for him, the publisher fees and editor's fees all paid up, that's about thirty grand. It's lifelong contracts for you, but he didn't want you to have to work to make this happen, so there is just over forty million in a holding account for you to do with as you please. Oh, and there is computer equipment in your office already." Robert looked at Tyler. "I said houses, not house. He had four of them, spread out all over the world. The one here, it's in bad repair and he kept it that way, he told me, to keep you boys coming around. It's set up now that it will be updated and remodeled when you're ready. Dominic, you have seventeen million in accounts for you to use, tuition to any Ivy League college you wish to attend as well. Any money you don't use for this goes back to you, in addition to extra that will round out to fifty million as well. Books, a car, housing, as well as a generous allowance for you to use. And a cash settlement. As I said, Arnold was a very generous man, and one that invested well in what he considered his family."

No one moved. Not even his father, who was the most animated person he'd ever seen. Robert turned to Caleb, his face set and his eyes full of mirth, and Caleb was almost afraid for him to speak. But when he opened his mouth, Caleb stopped him.

"I don't want to know." Robert said that he might not, but it wouldn't change things. "I'm assuming, from the amount of the gifts to my family, that Arnold was a very wealthy man."

"He was. His wife was as well. The acreage that he left to the pack is worth a great deal of money. And so you know, that reverts to you if Daniel or any other pack leader doesn't uphold his rules that he set forth." Caleb said it was too much. "No. To him it wasn't nearly enough. You gave him hope and family when he had none. All of you did that for him. Gave him something that he thought he'd never have. Love again."

"Do I have stipulations on the building?" Robert told him there was only one stipulation, but more than one building. "One thing at a time, please. And this stipulation, if I don't do it, what happens?"

"Nothing. The building will still be yours, but at a small cost. A dollar, in case you're wondering, but it's doubtful that you're going to renege on it. He wanted you to open your own firm. He thought you were being abused by the one you work for now, and he thought that you'd branch out if you had your own place." Caleb told him how he'd just quit his job on Friday. "Good. One less thing you must worry about now. Caleb, he left you a total of nineteen buildings, not including the one that he has set up for you. The total worth of them all isn't as much as it should be, but he figured that once you started working, others would want to revitalize the downtown area again. Your total worth right now is just over two point seven billion dollars."

~~~

Kelley sat down beside his oldest son. Caleb was just staring off into space, and Kelley didn't blame him. This was quite the bombshell. He said his name three times before his son turned to look at him.

"You okay?" He nodded, then shook his head. "Yeah, got that same reaction from your momma a few minutes ago. She's plum upset about this whole thing. Arnold, he sure did keep us in the dark about stuff. Not that it was any of our business what he had in his pocketbook, but to leave this all to us when.... Well, I'm not sure, but he sure did take care of us."

"He was rich." Kelley nodded. "And he...he made us all millionaires. Millionaires, Dad. And me? I'm a billionaire. We have more money right now that I ever expected to see in all my life. Why is Mom upset?"

Kelley laughed a little. These boys of his, they sure did take after him when it came to being sidetracked when their momma was concerned. He was right proud of them for that.

"She thinks he should have used the money for evil." Kelley laughed at the expression on his face. "I don't think she meant evil, but she said he should'a enjoyed his twilight years a little more than just hanging out with us."

"I think he loved us." Kelley knew that he did. He told Caleb that he loved him as well. "I have over a billion dollars in assets. Buildings that I have no idea what to do with. An office and staff. Plus, I'm unemployed."

"I don't think you're unemployed, son, if you have a staff. It don't rightly work that way." Caleb growled at him and Kelley laughed. "You gonna do it? Come here and run your own business? I gotta tell you, it's great to see you all getting this jumpstart to bring you home a bit more. Dominic is already planning to apply to colleges for his doctorate. Gabe is looking on that Internet thing for himself a nice house nearby. Tyler is talking to a contractor that Robert set up for him. I think Xander is making notes on a book. An actual book he wants to write. Owen.... Well, he's just sitting there holding onto that watch of Arnold's. Nice thing to do, to give him that busted one. I think it means more to him than the others might."

"Did you have any idea that he was worth even a tenth

of that, Dad?" He shook his head, but said that it really didn't surprise him. "Why not? I mean, I can remember just about every meal he ate with us. How many times he was here just to hang around. Why did he live around here when he could have been anywhere else in the world?"

"He had friends here. People like us, mostly you, who talked to him. Treated him like a regular Joe instead of some rich man who they wanted to sucker. Would we have treated him different like? I think so. We would have stayed away. Might not have gone fishing so much. And I'm pretty sure we wouldn't have had him in our home. Might have thought it wasn't good enough for a man like him. But we didn't do nary a thing but to treat him just like what he was to us. A good friend." Caleb nodded. "Thanks to him, you got yourself a good start on doing something you wanna do. Us too. But you, you got a lot of money to do whatever you want. What will it be, son?"

"I'm going to go to the office he set up for me in the morning. See about getting some clients. The best part is, I guess I won't have to be broke and can take my time in getting things ready." Kelley asked him what else. "Close down my apartment...I don't know. I have so many things just buzzing around that I can't even keep them all straight."

"Good. That's what it should be. Your head working things out first before you go and spend willy nilly. I know you won't, but I'm glad to see that being a billionaire didn't change you much." Kelley was still laughing when he walked away.

Kelley and his Sara still had all the boys' rooms like they had left them. Caleb had shared his room with his brother Gabe when they were younger, and now was no different. But instead of going to bed, like maybe had been his plan, Kelley knew that his son was going to sit down at the old computer and began pulling up real-estate sites. Yes sirree bob, it was sure nice to have his boys home.

~~~

By the time Gabe came to bed at around midnight, Caleb had a list of houses, a better idea of where his new offices might be, as well as the several other buildings that he owned. He asked Gabe what his plan was going to be now.

"Don't know, actually. I mean, I could pretty much do whatever I want, but all I find myself doing is missing the old man." Caleb said he did as well. "We would have been at his house today. Hanging out, more than likely having a fish fry one more time before the cold weather set in."

"More than likely he would have been out there with us while we closed his barn, and winterized his mower and tractor. I'm still in shock that he's gone. I know that he was old, but I thought he'd be around forever." Gabe nodded and smiled sadly. "This money? I have no idea what I'm supposed to do now."

"What he wanted us to do, I think. You know as well as I that we've both been bitching about being home more and having a place here to call our own. I don't just mean a house, but business too. It's been difficult for me, all the traveling, and for little recognition from the group I work with. Being a country doctor and low man on the pole sure does make for some shitty calls. I know you've felt the same way." Caleb told him how many emails he'd gotten from Lancaster since Friday. "See? He knows that he's screwed up in treating you like shit, and now that you're going to open your own place, he'll go under in no time."

"I liked working for his dad. He was funny. Gave credit where it was due. And if you messed up, and I did a lot those

42

first few months there, he would take you aside, talk it over with you, and offer up some tidbit of help that would get you through. His son is an asshole and a prick. Several times since he took over, I caught him taking credit for my design. It's why I sign everything now."

"We all needed this. Including Mom and Dad." Caleb nodded. "Are you going into town in the morning? If so, I'd like to hang out with you while you do some looking around. I need to have an office here if I'm going to open my practice, and I might as well use one of yours if you're willing to rent to me."

"You won't pay me rent, Gabe. I'll gladly give you whatever you want in the way of offices. I'd rather you do something for yourself with whatever rent you might pay out…save it for a nice vacation. Or you could put it to a house of your own." Caleb would show him the four houses he was looking at, as well as the buildings, tomorrow. "We can both figure out which ones we want and then have lunch in town. I'm thinking…I was hoping we could spread a little of this around the town. Revitalize it a little."

"Sounds like a plan." They talked until the wee hours of the morning. By six-thirty, the time that his parents were up and about, both had taken a shower, dressed, and were armed with lists. Caleb had another list, one that he hadn't shared with his brother, that he was going to take care of as well. He was going to upgrade and remodel his parents' home.

He knew they'd not move, so this was a good plan. And he was sure that his brothers would want to help out too. They needed to have this as much as he needed to give it to them.

CHAPTER 3

"Dad? You wanted to see me?" Quinn sat down in the chair across from her dad's desk and blew her bangs out of her face. "There is no end to the fuckery going on around here today. Did you actually tell two people that you were going to have a baby?"

"I did. It was funny. I love going for the shock value with people." Quinn shook her head. Her dad was...well, he was the best there was. "I got an email with mock ups from Lancaster. Speaking of fuckery, that man has it in spades. He said that the drawings that he sent me were from one of his other brilliant artists, as Caleb is on vacation."

"Vacation? During our contract with them? How is that even possible for them to...? Okay, I can see it, but what are we going to do now?" Her dad leaned back in his seat, the smile all over his face. "What did you do?"

"I didn't do anything. But Caleb is no more on vacation than I am. He's quit." Quinn felt the shock race over her. And the dread. They'd have to start from scratch on this thing. "Lancaster is in breach of contract as of right now."

"How do you know that this guy quit? Last time we spoke with Lancaster, he said that the two of them were going to be our men in this, and that Caleb was going to be a full partner because of the work he's done before." Her dad just shook his head. "Dad, we have a lot of money resting on this new product going out with a bang. Without Caleb there, we're pretty much fucked on this."

"No, I don't think so. First of all, I know for sure because I called to speak to him and the woman that answered the phone said that he was no longer there. Then when I called back, asked to be directed to Lancaster, he told me this cock and bull story about him being on vacation, there had been a death in his family."

"Was there?" He told her about the close friend who had died. "So he quit over that? I don't think I like where this is going with this firm. Or this Winchester person."

"Lancaster, according to my source, went to Caleb on Friday at about eight-thirty that evening, and told him that he needed him to stay and finish a project. It was ours." Quinn asked why Lancaster had waited until then. "That I haven't been able to find out, but Caleb was on his way out the door and Lancaster threatened him with his job if he didn't stay. So, he quit. There is more to this story, I'm sure, but I'm still working on it."

"So Lancaster, for whatever reason, waits until the guy is literally walking out the door before he throws our project at him. I don't know that I'd not walk too. That's a shitty thing to do on a Friday. Not to mention.... What was the deadline on that for them?" Her dad told her. "It was due Friday? And he waited until then to talk to him about it? Why? He's had the stuff for nearly three weeks, Dad."

"I know. And so you know, I called him to ask him where it was. He didn't say what the delay was, because I had no idea about the rest of this. But I told him I needed it by the end of day on Monday. The email I got from him...let me check."

While her dad checked the timestamp, Quinn tried to think how the fuck they were going to push a new product when they had not the first thing done about advertising. Lancaster Advertising had even agreed to make their label on this. Now they had shit. No printable cover for the cans and bags that the product was going to go in. Nothing for the newspapers, the news, nor the flyers that were going to be handed out. The dog food, an all-natural dog food that was going to be out in three months, was at a complete standstill until they got what they needed from Lancaster.

"I got it as seven o'clock on Monday night. Here, let me read you the email that is attached. This will get your hair all knotted up. 'Mr. Dorsey. I do hope that you like what we've been able to put together for you. It is some of our top work. One of my most brilliant personnel and I worked on this for the entire weekend. We look forward to hearing from you soon.' Then it goes on to talk about how they can have the proofs to me in three weeks."

She took the printed-up mocks that her dad handed her. Quinn looked at her dad then back at the drawings. There wasn't any way that this had come from the hand of Winchester, and if this other guy was brilliant, she'd hate to see what he thought of as terrible. She'd seen Winchester's work and knew it like her own hand.

"It looks like he got a kindergartener to do this. I mean, there aren't even any of the colors we normally use. No puppy on the younger dog food. There isn't any mention that there are no preservatives or corn products." Her dad nodded. "Dad, this is all so wrong. We need to get someone else now. If not, we're going to be sitting on a great deal of ideas with no one to buy them."

"I have a plan." She groaned. "What a way to talk to your

dad. You know me and plans. They usually work out well."

"Usually being the operative word there. What is your plan, and how am I going to fix this with you?" She didn't care for the grin he showed her. "Dad? What are you thinking?"

"Caleb is a short two-hour drive from here." She nodded, not sure she liked where she thought this was going. "I'm thinking we need a road trip. You, me, and your brother drive out there, see if we can talk him into doing this for us, and maybe convince him that he needs to open a firm of his own."

"Why on earth would you think he'd jump at that? I know I wouldn't." He cocked his brow at her. "Okay, I wouldn't have left it undone in the first place. What makes you think this guy, Winchester, is going to want to do anything for us after this? Or for that matter, why should we even ask him to?"

He tossed her a file, one that she'd seen before. The very file that she had seen when he'd told her about Lancaster Advertising and Caleb Winchester. She opened it up, ready to tell him she'd seen this before, when the top sheet of paper took her breath away.

"He did this?" Her dad was saying something about mock ups and other firms, but she was focused on the drawing and not paying attention.

The advertising was for a brand of lettuce sold in a bag. There was nothing special about the product itself. Lettuce, carrots, and a few darker greens put in the bag for show. She knew what they were…it was her main staple in life when it came to cooking at home. Grab a bag, a bottle of dressing, and voila, dinner was served. But he'd gone beyond that.

He'd hit all the three must haves in advertising in a single photo that didn't need any other words but the bag on the table. The bag that the lettuce had come in was laying on a table, sort of like a table cloth, she supposed. The bowl that the greens were in was clear, the different colors in the bowl there for the eye to see. The product placement was superb. Cherry tomatoes and a few sunflower seeds were laying on the table, ready to be put into it, which would wake the taste buds. A person's hands were grating cheese from a block over it…the photo caught the small flakes as they fell onto the lettuce. Hitting another highlight in advertising, versatility in a product. Convenience was the final add-in. Just open the bag, add a few things, and you were done. She loved every part of this. Quinn looked up at her dad when he laughed.

"He was having dinner with a friend of his…might have been related, I'm not sure. But anyway, I asked if I could join them. Both men were very nice, spoke well of the area, and they said how they'd just lost someone dear to them. A family friend." She asked her dad how he'd managed to get this. "Hold your horses. You always wanted the punchline to a joke well before I was ready to tell it. Anyway, after telling him I was sorry for his loss, this picture slides out of the folder they had between them. So being me, I asked about it. You know what he said? Told me that a bit ago, he'd been watching television—something that he never does, mind you—and he saw this ad for that brand of salad. Caleb said how he'd thought the man could have done better, by saying a lot less and just showing."

"I saw that commercial. There is a guy who is narrating it. Nasal voice that made me think of nails on a chalkboard. Open the bag, he says, pour it into a bowl. Then he goes on and on about adding shit. Like chicken, tomatoes, even cheese. I lost interest in it because his voice was annoying me so much that I wanted to punch him in the throat." Her dad nodded. "Did he say that to the man?"

"No, he was much politer, believe it or not. He said he told the man that he should just let the product—in this case a salad in a bowl—speak for itself. I guess Caleb spent like twenty minutes with the man, showed him how to set it up, even had a photographer go and take some snaps. That's what he called them too, snaps. Who talks like that? Anyway, he took the pictures and showed them to a test group. They loved it over the nasal speaker. And sales went up four and a half percent overnight. After a month? They're up by nearly sixty percent." Quinn looked at the picture, then at her dad, asking him the cost. When he laughed again, she smiled. "Nothing. Not one penny. He said that his aunt liked the salad, but had to mute the commercial when it came on because of something that the man was saying bothered her."

"The voice." Dad said he didn't say that, of course, but he told him that was it. "Twenty minutes, Dad. This guy did this work in twenty minutes. And here we sit waiting on the same guy to help us for over a month, and nothing to show for it."

"Precisely why we need to go and see him. If he is opening his own firm, we need to get in on the ground floor, or at least at the top of the list." She asked about Lancaster. "He didn't meet his obligations to us. Breach of contract, as I said."

Quinn was tempted. More than that, she wanted to go now by herself and beg him to take them on. Instead, she sat there with her dad and made arrangements to get Harley ready to go with them. He would enjoy the road trip for no other reason than he could be in a car. Her brother loved riding in a car more than he did chocolate chip cookies.

By the time she was ready to go for the day, not only had they made arrangements at the local hotel, but had called ahead to arrange a few outings for Harley. She was getting excited and knew that this was going to be the thing they needed. She just hoped that Caleb Winchester was as nice as he was good. She wouldn't take his shit if he wasn't, not for any amount of sales because of his work.

~~~

"Where do you want this?" Caleb looked at his dad and counted to ten. "You should just let it out, your momma sure has been. I tell you, I think it was easier moving you to college than it's been getting this here office ready to go."

"I don't know where I want anything. I only came here to look around and see what I needed. But since I opened the doors, all kinds of things have been brought in." He sat down at the desk, the only piece of furniture that he knew was unwrapped. "There is too much going on for me. I'm overwhelmed."

His dad set the box down that held a filing cabinet. Caleb had no idea if he should put it in here or out in the main part of the building. He'd never had one before working for Lancaster. His dad moved to the corner of the room and got a bottle of water out of the cooler that Caleb's mom had brought in. As he unscrewed the top, he looked around at the mess.

"I'm thinking that these here delivery people had this on hold, and as soon as they saw you, decided to get it off their books." He sat down on a box as he went on with his theory. "You thinking that you got too much, or you just ain't used to having so much?"

"Both I guess. The phone has been ringing off the hook since I plugged it in. Mom is the running man on those for me. It's all people who have things for this building. They're making arrangements to bring them here. Most of them are even instructed to put whatever it is together for me as well." His dad nodded. "I thought about just having it put on the upper floor of the place, but I went up there to get away and

51

decided that I want that for my drawing room. It's filled with light, with all the windows. Dad, this place is perfect for what I have in mind."

"Maybe that's why Arnold picked it for you. We'll move your desk up there in a bit. I wanted to talk to you anyway. You know how to run a business? I mean, not yours, but these that Arnold gave us? I worked for him for a spell, but not in the factories. It was more like I interviewed some fellers to do grunt work. Heck fire, son. I know less about factories than I do about tinkering with that recording thing we got with the cable company." He asked his dad what he meant. "He went and left us three companies. You know, I had to go and look them up. They're huge, did you know that?"

"Yes. I mean, I didn't before, but I did after...like you, I looked them up. But I don't really think you're going to be required to run them, as in going into the office and making out schedules or anything like that. Mostly just make decisions when they ask and keep an eye on things. They're pretty well established, and Robert said that he'd help you." His dad nodded, but Caleb could tell he wasn't satisfied with just that. "I'm sure that if you wanted to take an active role in the running, you could do that easily."

"I can. I was reading up on the one that manufactures mats. You know, the kind that kiddies use on the floor at nap time. In my day, we didn't take naps but worked, but I ain't the one in charge of schools." Caleb had to cover his mouth so his dad wouldn't see him laughing. "Anyway, I want to see what they do, mostly. I don't need to run it just yet, but I'd like to learn the hows and the why tos of it."

"Do you plan to go in and change things? To be honest with you, Dad, I'd steer clear of that. Like you said, you don't know anything about it yet." His dad said that was the point.

"You mean you want to learn it to make improvements?"

"Nah, I'm not that smart, but when somebody asks me what it is I do for a living, I wanna be able to have a halfway decent answer. Like 'I make kiddy mats,' that ain't no answer." Again, he was careful not to laugh at his dad. It wasn't laughing at him, but more that he enjoyed his dad's simple way of thinking things. "You can say to somebody, 'I make pretty pictures of food and stuff so that people like you will wanna buy it.' Me, I make mats and money. See the difference?"

"I do. And I understand. I'd call up Robert though, and have him make the arrangements. The new owner showing up out of the blue will make people nervous." His dad said that was good to know. "Also, if you're going to learn the business, why not take a few weeks and go there to actually do it? You might enjoy that too."

"I might. I just might do that." His dad got up and picked up the box he'd been carrying when he came in. "I'm thinking that with all these men here, we can get this done lickety split. I'll go and talk to a couple of them big guys and we'll get this desk right where you want it."

An hour later, not only was his desk on the upper floor, but he'd figured out where to put some of the filing cabinets too. He stored them against the wall in the room he'd been occupying earlier. By the end of the day, they had all the boxes empty and cleared out, his office set up the way he wanted it, and there were shades on all the windows on the main floor. All in all, he thought it was a very productive day. But he was tired and still needed to go and look at a couple more houses. He wasn't thrilled with the three that he and Gabe had looked at. They were too far from his mom and dad, and they didn't make him feel like it was going to be a home. They were...he supposed they were just houses. Caleb wanted a home.

He decided to forgo having to make his own dinner and hit the local restaurant. They had the best burgers he'd ever eaten and sweet potato fries, one of his all-time favorite junk foods. As soon as he entered the place, he could sense something was wrong.

The screaming had his wolf tingling along his skin, not like he needed to protect him, but to protect whoever the person was that seemed to be upset. Making his way to the table, he told himself he was just making sure no one was hurt. But seeing the young man there with someone that looked familiar, he knew what was happening. Instead of getting upset like most of the other patrons were, he sat down across from the younger man and snapped his fingers in front of his face. It had the desired effect and he looked at him.

"What's wrong?" The young man, about twenty he thought, started rocking back and forth and moaning. "Come on, you can tell me, can't you?"

"He doesn't care for the fries." He looked over at the man, trying his best to place him. "I met you the other day, in here. This is my son, Harley. He's nonverbal autistic. My daughter is usually with me when we go out, but she got called away a bit ago."

Putting out his hand, Caleb waiting to see if Harley would take it or not. When he laid his hand in his and turned away, Caleb gave it a brief squeeze and waited. The returning squeeze made him smile. Then he turned and looked at him.

"Hello there." Harley rocked more but not as hard. "My name is Caleb. I know your dad. Can you show me what's wrong with your fries?"

They were shoved at him and he looked them over. They looked all right to him, but he knew that with people like

Harley, it wouldn't be obvious to anyone but him. Harley's dad explained what it was.

"They're too light. I know that sounds silly, but when I cook them for him at home, I usually get distracted and I toast them up a little. He usually isn't any trouble when we go out. I feel just horrible for making a scene." Caleb told him not to worry about it. "Well, I just don't like to upset anyone."

An elderly woman huffed at them. "Some people are trying to enjoy a nice meal, not having to listen to this. People like him should be put away."

Caleb stood up. "Put away? What if they started putting everyone away, as you suggested, that was having a bad day? I'm thinking you'd have been locked up years ago. Why don't you move along now and stop interfering with what we're doing? There is nothing going on here that concerns you."

When she moved along, huffing a great deal more, Caleb sat back down. Harley took his hand again and he held it. Calling for Angel, the waitress, he explained to her what they needed.

"Can you pop them back in again for him? Just toast them up a little more." She nodded and winked at him. "Thanks, sweetie. And tell your momma I said hi."

The man sat down. "I'm Alexander Dorsey. I own Dorsey Products." Caleb started to explain about Lancaster. "He emailed me some shit, claiming that you did it."

"I don't work there any longer. He and I had a falling out about something." Caleb thought about the man's product. "I'm sorry, but I had a death in the family. I couldn't work on it without more notice."

"He had it for weeks. Never heard a thing from him, so I called him. I'm thinking about the time you had walked out." Angel brought the fresh fries, telling them to be careful, they were hot, and Caleb told Harley. "You're good with him. I'm guessing you either have someone in your family like him or a friend."

"My brother is a special needs teacher. I go in a couple of times a month and help with art projects and stuff. Before I could, however, he had me take a few classes that would prepare me. I don't think I've ever had a better time than I do in his classroom." Alexander nodded and watched his son eat his now toasty fries. "He's doing really well. Better than a lot of kids that I've worked with."

"His sister. My Quinn said that she would give up college to help him function. Harley's mom died giving him life, and when the doctors suggested that I put him in a nice little home, couldn't do it. Not just me, Quinn couldn't either. We get help with him, but he's family and we all stick it out." Caleb said he could understand that. "I bet you can. I've been doing some reading up on you. I'm to understand that you're opening your own place up."

"Yes. I mean I plan on it. It's still in the planning stages. Though you'd never know that to see the place." Alexander asked him what he meant. "Arnold—he was the man we lost recently—he set me up with a place, furniture, as well as some cash. I never expected it. It was a Godsend, but it wasn't anything I would have ever thought he'd do. Every day I miss him more."

"I read about him. He was a good man." Caleb asked if he knew him. "Not in a social setting, but yes, I knew him. Like I said, he was a good man. A better friend to you too, I'm guessing."

"Yes." Caleb ordered him and Harley a burger after getting permission from his dad. "Dominic is going back to school for his doctorate. He figures with his life study classes and the ones he's taken online, he should be a doctor of special needs education in about eighteen months or less. I'm betting the less part will be more to his style of doing things. He is really good with kids like your son. He runs a sort of day camp about four times a year, along with a bunch of other men and woman that he works with. They have a good time. There are horses that are trained to handle them. A few ducks at a pond, fishing, and some other activities too. If you'd like, I can see if he can get Harley in. It's the least I can do to make up for failing you on the project."

"I'd like that. But I don't think you failed me. Not if we can work something out between us. I still want you to do this for me. Quinn and I do. She's my partner. But if you could just give us a few hours of your time so we can go over it, I think you can do us a world of good." Alexander smiled. "Also, I'd very much like for you to see about the camp for Harley. I think he'll enjoy it a great deal. He has one at home that he goes to, but they mostly make them work on projects inside. Not a lot of room for them to go wandering around. Also, we've decided that the ratio between campers and helpers isn't nearly enough for what kind of needs they have."

"I think they have one person, sometimes two, to each camper. That's why it's harder to get into the program. And I know that they have a good staff. I've worked there as well, when I can. My brother doesn't run the program, but he does have a hand in a lot of the things they do."

"I'm glad to know that. It sounds like a place he'd enjoy. Like I mentioned, he doesn't get out much, not unless he's at home." Caleb finished his burger and gave Harley the rest of his fries. "He usually doesn't take well to strangers. I'm glad to see that you don't have an aversion to his needs."

"Never. Everyone is a person, and just because he's not

like me, doesn't mean we can't be friends." Alexander thanked him. "There isn't any reason to thank me. I just wanted to help."

"Well, I do thank you. You saved me from leaving and never returning." Alexander laughed a little. "I'm glad to meet you anyway, under less than nefarious conditions."

Nodding, Caleb wasn't sure but he thought that he'd been highjacked. He wasn't even ready to pull out a sheet of paper or get his cameras set up, all new in the building, and he was talking to a potential new client. He tried to calm himself by not thinking and holding Harley's hand, but he was sick nervous about it all.

CHAPTER 4

Quinn wasn't sure this was a good idea. She had no idea how she'd let her dad talk her into sending her brother to this camp. Harley didn't know any of these people, and neither did she. Yes, they'd done a lot of research on the place and the list of people that Dominic had given her and her dad, but still, Harley was her little brother. As he made his way to the group of men and women that were standing in a circle, she made sure again that he had all the things that had been required of them. A woman walked up to them and introduced herself as Debra Manning just as Harley took off running for the group of like young men.

"He'll be fine. No one will let him venture far." Quinn told her that he'd never done anything like this before. "Most of them haven't. We take on a few new people every year. It's a long waiting list. Caleb—he's Dominic's brother—has never asked to have someone come in before. I think that's why we all said yes so quickly."

"I don't know if this is a good idea. He's lived with my dad and me his whole life. We have help, but this is very strange to him." They both looked over at Harley, who was laughing and touching one of the other people there. "I guess maybe it's just me, then."

She laughed with Debra. "He'll be fine. James and I are going to be his buddies at the camp. Each child is assigned one or two people to help. That's why we take so few kids. There is a doctor on staff, plus all of us are versed in not just CPR, but we've gone through a great many classes in how to work with special needs people."

Quinn was feeling better and better as she spoke to Debra. As she told her more about the camp, she watched her brother. One of the men started to wander away, but he was brought back to the group with a gentle hand and laughter. He didn't get upset by being brought back, nor did he run again. Quinn looked at Debra.

"I think he'll be fine. I'll be a basket case until he returns, but I think he'll be okay there." Debra handed her a card and Quinn handed her one of hers. "You can call me at any time. I never go anywhere without my phone."

"If you call me, I might not answer you. We try hard not to take away from the kids when we're with them. But if you leave a message, I'll get back to you sometime within twenty-four hours." Quinn told her that would be great. "I promise you, he'll be just fine."

As the bus pulled away, she felt tears fill her eyes as he waved at her from his seat. Quinn waved back, blowing him kisses when he did the same to her. She was going to miss him, but hoped more than anything that he had a good time.

Driving back to the house that her dad and she had rented for the month, she thought of the meeting that she was going to have with Caleb Winchester tonight. She'd met and talked with his brother, Dominic, and found that that he was one of six sons of Kelley and Sara Winchester. They'd gone to Caleb's new offices as well, just to look around, and she was very impressed. There were a lot of people in the building, so they were told that they could have a look around, but to stay out of the way.

State of the art everything, including the coffee machine. There was a large drafting table that could easily sit three people. Shelves of paper in all colors were stacked in neat rows. Filing cabinets made especially for draft paper. There was a large printer, big enough to print out poster sized photos quickly and beautifully. She was impressed with the cameras, each of them with a large lens. Pens and inks of every imaginable color. Quinn felt her hands itch to touch any and all of the things in the place, and she knew next to nothing about how to use them.

Her dad was in his room getting dressed for a meeting when her cell rang. Not recognizing the number, she answered cautiously. There was a great deal of noise at the other end. It sounded to her like a bus station or an airport. Before she could begin to think this was a wrong number and hang up, a man spoke quickly and urgently.

"It's David Lancaster. I've been trying to reach Alexander Dorsey. Is he around?" She sat down and thought of all the things she could say to this man, none of them very nice. "Are you there? Damn it. I think I lost the call again."

"No, you didn't. I'm here. Although I'm not sure why you'd want to speak to either of us at this point. I think you've heard from our attorneys." The man spoke, but she had a feeling it wasn't to her. Something about how he had it, whatever that might mean. "My father and I made it perfectly clear that we've gone elsewhere for our work."

"You can't do that to us." She started to explain how she'd done nothing, he had, but he spoke again. "I've been talking things over with Caleb, and he's coming back to work for us. There was a slight misunderstanding between us."

61

"You said he was on vacation, I believe. Now you're saying that he doesn't work for you?" He cursed again, low and very fluently. "And I doubt very much you've spoken to him lately. Mr. Winchester is now working for us. So, as I know that this conversation is over, let me give you a piece of advice. I don't think you should lie to any of your future clients, Mr. Lancaster. It's very unprofessional. Not to mention rude."

"What the fuck do you mean, he's working for you? He can't do that. I have a contract with you. You're going to stop this right now. I won't have you going behind my back like this." She laughed because he'd completely missed the point of her advice. Quinn could almost feel his anger through the connection. "Look, I think we got off on the wrong footing. We've both made some mistakes and we can resolve this right now. I'll get Caleb to come back and work for me, and you'll reinstate the retainer that you had with my company. I can't believe you did that in the first place, but now that we've worked it out between us, you'll have to put that back in the bank. That's better for all of us. I'd really hate to have to take you to court over all of this when we can just settle it like good friends."

"Actually, I think the way things have turned out is going to be better for us all. We are not friends, by the way…we were going to be client to client. You will just have to look elsewhere for another consumer to screw over. We're finished. And if you threaten my firm with an attorney again, I will have your ass for breakfast." She stood up when she heard her dad laughing. "The next time you call me, it had better be because you're apologizing."

She disconnected the call and stared at her dad, who was laughing pretty hard by then. Stretching her neck, she heard it pop twice before she could speak. Sitting down, she let out a long breath and decided that she could have easily broken about a dozen things.

"He try and get you to change our mind?" She told him what Lancaster had said to her. "Damned fool. You'd think that after the conversation that Billings had with him this morning, he'd be fine with this. I had him break all ties and make sure that he understood we had gone elsewhere because he'd broken our contract."

"The man is an idiot. I'm surprised that anyone would want to work for him, much less have his firm do any kind of work. Christ, he actually threatened me. Me? What the fuck is wrong with people?" Her dad laughed again. "What time do we meet with Winchester? Soon, I hope. I need to get things rolling."

"In two hours. We're meeting him at his parents' home. Mrs. Winchester called here about an hour ago and asked if we could. Caleb is still in the process of finding a home, and the restaurant in town is closed today, she told me, and she wanted to meet us anyway." Quinn asked how many were going to be there as she got up to work some of the soreness out of her leg. "The entire family, I guess. Also, not that either of us care, but they're wolves."

"Shifter?" Quinn felt the hair on her arms dance. And when her dad nodded at her, she sat down, trying her best not to look as terrified as she felt. "They're all shifters, or just him?"

"All of them. I guess they're purebloods too. Are you all right?" Her head was spinning and she had to run. Not just run, but hide as well. Shifters. Quinn was terrified of shifters, especially wolves. "Quinn, look at me."

"He was just there, in the shadows. And then he jumped

out at me and I felt his teeth sink into me." She was breathing hard, making no sense, she knew. Quinn could feel her heart pounding in her chest, even hear her hard breaths as she tried to control it. It wasn't until she felt the sting on her face that she stared up at her dad and knew that she'd frightened him. So much so that he'd slapped her to bring her around. "I was hurt a few days ago. A wolf, he chased me around the parking garage at the mall until he cornered me. I wasn't hurt that bad, only a few stitches, but it was enough to give me nightmares."

"Why didn't you tell me?" Quinn told him she didn't want to worry him. "Well, believe it or not, that's my job. Oh, honey, you should have told me. I could have been there for you. First thing, we're going to take care of this as soon as we get home. I won't have my daughter harmed by someone. I don't care what I have to do. And we're going home right now."

"We most certainly are not leaving. I will muscle through this, and if Winchester gives me a hard time or even looks like he's going to shift and bother me, I will pull out a gun and shoot his nuts off." Her dad stared at her for a full ten seconds before he started laughing. "Dad, really, I'm all right. Afraid, yes, but I'll be all right."

"You don't have to go to this meeting if you'd rather not. I mean, I might not have agreed to going to their home either if they hadn't been so nice in getting Harley in that camp." She said that was nice of them. "Look, let's just go there with an open mind, and we'll decide if we want to do this. I think he's the best, but I won't have him scaring my number one little girl."

"I'm your only girl, Dad." She went to take a shower and get ready. She was going to go with an open mind and her mouth shut. Laughing, she knew that the latter part was never going to happen, but she would be opened minded.

Looking down at her leg, she wondered if she should have mentioned that it was sore still. That she was sure that there was something wrong with the bite. And the bruising around it hadn't gone away either. Quinn decided that as soon as she got home, she was seeing someone about it. Even if she had to see another wolf for answers. This wasn't normal and she knew it.

~~~

Caleb wasn't sure this was a good idea. He'd gotten two phone calls today from the Lancaster firm, and he was sure that he was going to be in deep shit. He'd asked Robert his opinion on the matter, and he told him he'd look into things. But there was still the call from David that bothered him a lot more than he wanted it to.

"You fucking traitor." It had taken him a few moments to realize who it was when David continued. "You actually went behind my back and contacted the Dorsey firm? And then set yourself up as their advertising firm when I was willing to take you back? How could you do that to me? After all I've done for you."

"What is it you think you've done for me, David? Make me work all hours on projects that were shoved to the side until the last minute? And only remembered them when the client called to ask about them? I could have done a better job on a lot of those projects if you had given me more time." He asked if Caleb had given him shitty work. "Never, and you know that. Otherwise you would have been out of business long ago. What does your dad think about how poorly you're running his company? I bet he's thrilled to death that he's left it to someone that snorts all profits up his nose every day."

"Who told you that? Margaret? It's all lies, all of whatever she told you." Caleb knew that David was a cokehead, he could smell it on him all the time. "You're going to come back and work for me, Caleb, or I'll ruin you. Do you hear me? I will stop at nothing to ruin you."

"Caleb?" He turned and looked at his mom, her voice pulling him from his thoughts. Horrible thoughts, as a matter of fact. "Here, let me do it. You and your father. I've never seen two more alike men when it came to tying a tie."

"I'm thinking that with my new firm, I'm only going to wear polo shirts with my company name on them. All the time. I think it will save me money on dry-cleaning, as well as time spent in front of a mirror trying to make one of these things work." In less time than it would have taken him to tie his shoes, Mom had him looking good. "Thank you. Not just for making me presentable, but with this dinner thing too. I'm sure that they have a butt load of servants that cook for them all the time, but they'll never have a dinner like you're making. What are you making, anyway?"

"Liver and onions," she laughed. Caleb was sure that the look on his face said it all about liver and onions. "We're having a beef roast and all the trimmings. And Sally Anne made us a blueberry pie for dessert. I tell you, that family could make a fortune baking like they do."

"You remember the Tomlinson building?" She stared at him, her eyes bright with understanding. "If you can talk them into renting it from me, I'll help them with their logo and advertising. Also.... Well, I'm not sure what the going rate is for rent, but they can rent it for six months...a year with no rent, so long as they can show that they're making a profit each month."

"You'd do that?" Caleb kissed her on the forehead and said that he would. "I think it's a brilliant idea. They'll be hard to convince, but I think I can do it."

"Mom, I have all the faith in the world in you doing it." She slapped him playfully on the chest. "Besides, someone gave me a chance...I'd like to pay it forward a bit and help out someone else. Maybe they'll build up a few extra jobs for the area."

By the time they were gathered in the living room awaiting their guests, not only did Caleb have a logo in mind for the new bakery, but he had an entire series of bags and wall designs in mind. He was just talking his mom into letting him take some pictures of her hands in some flour when his dad yelled that they had company. Caleb took several pictures of his mom working in the kitchen before he went to the front door. Mr. Dorsey looked completely out of his element with all his family standing there.

"You are a big family, aren't you?" Caleb introduced them all to him and then Mr. Dorsey hugged his mom. "My goodness, you don't look nearly old enough to have sons this old. I thought for sure you were an aunt or something."

"Thank you. But they're mine. Somedays I'd like to give them away, then they go and make up for it by doing something nice for someone. Sometimes me, but not always. Welcome to our home, Mr. Dorsey. But I thought your daughter was coming too."

"She's here. There was a phone call about one of our lines in the factory that she's fixing. When she turned sixteen, she decided that she wanted to know the ins and outs of the production line. Good thing she did too. We learned a lot from her month there. Lowered our production cost by three percent, and helped us cut out some duplicate work that saved us a bit too. Smart girl, my Quinn." His dad told him how he wanted to do that. "You should do it. I'm telling you right now, you won't regret it. Why, I go down and work the line myself when I'm thinking I'm too big for my britches. Humbles a man to walk in another man's shoes."

They made their way to the living room, talking about how things worked in his factory compared to the one that his dad had inherited. Caleb would bet anything that the two of them would be planning a hunting trip by the end of the night.

He looked out the window and saw the woman on the phone. She was talking with her hands moving a great deal, her hair blowing wildly in the evening breeze. He couldn't see her face, but he'd bet she was pretty. And her body was nice too. She worked out, that he noticed as well.

"Have you talked to her yet?" He told Dominic that he'd not. "She's a looker, as Dad would say, and very smart. She asked questions about the camp that I don't think anyone ever thought of before."

"Like what?" Caleb watched her as Dominic told him. "I can see that. Paint can be toxic to some kids, and she was smart to ask that. And the blankets that you use are all new. That, to me, is a really nice touch that you give them to the kids when they leave. She all right with that part?"

"Yes. I told her that we make sure each person is seen by a doctor and someone signs off on their health before we even agree to take them in. Also, she asked and I told her that we have allergy pens, as well as a certified doctor on staff at the camp should they need someone. Also, that the helipad is always on standby, in the event that we need it."

Caleb watched her when she put her phone in her pocket. She was stiff with what he could only assume was anger. And when she screamed, just threw back her head and let out a sound that made birds fly from the trees, he laughed. She was one scary woman, he thought.

She paced the yard for ten minutes. He didn't mean to stare at her, though it was nice to see someone moving like she was. It was fluid, and had he had his camera he might have taken a few pictures of her while she worked off some steam. He'd not tell her of course. He had a feeling that it would piss her off more than she already was. When she turned to the house and headed up the porch, he was standing there waiting for her.

As soon as she came in the room he could smell it. Wolf. An alpha. Caleb stepped back, then took another couple of steps when she turned and looked at him. His mind went in all sorts of directions as she stood there, and none of them were good. When the door behind her closed completely, causing a small breeze to come his way, he could smell something else. Her scent.

"There you are, darling. Everything all right at home?" Her dad kissed her on her cheek and Caleb felt his wolf run over his skin.

Caleb looked at his brother Xander when he said his name. Before he could tell him anything, even one of the million and a half things that were running in his head, Caleb knew the exact moment that Xander smelled the other wolf as well. Both of them backed up more and hit the wall behind them when the woman came toward them.

"Caleb? What's wrong?" He couldn't tear his eyes away from the woman. And when her dad asked again what was wrong, he stood in front of her. That pissed his wolf off even more. He wanted to shift, hunt down the other wolf and kill him. Caleb had found his mate and she belonged to an alpha.

"What the hell is — ?"

Xander snapped at her. "Don't move. Don't fucking

move." She stopped, her foot settling back on the floor slowly. "You've been marked. And he's an alpha."

"Marked? I don't know what you mean." She looked at him then back at his brother. "Perhaps you'd better explain this to me. Right now, I want to hit you both."

"You could, but if you touch either of us, we're going to shift." She backed up. Xander laughed tightly. "Thank you. Where is your mate? The man who claimed you?"

"I don't know what you mean. I don't have a man in my life." Xander looked at Caleb, looking as confused as he was. "What's going on here? You invited us here, and now you're acting strangely. What do you mean, alpha and someone claiming me?"

"Honey, you were bitten." She looked at her dad when he spoke, and Caleb wanted to hurt him too. Not as badly as the other male, but it was close. "The wolf you were telling me about. He marked you."

"I don't know what that means." Xander started to explain, but she cut him off. "I was bitten yes, but I don't know who he was. He chased me all over the parking garage a few days ago, and when he cornered me by a parked car, he lunged and bit me. I saw a doctor and had it cleaned."

"It won't matter. He bit you and his saliva is in your body." Caleb cleared his throat, trying his best to calm his inner beast. "He might have a good reason for having bitten you, but the fact that you don't know him and he let you get away makes me think that he did it for sport."

"And that matters to you or me how?"

Caleb was in pain from keeping a distance from his mate. He didn't know what to do, but he could tell that the longer he stalled the angrier she got. And when her dad put his arm around her shoulders, Caleb let his beast growl.

"She's my mate, Mr. Dorsey. And I want you to step away from her before I hurt you." She stepped forward, her body hard once again in anger. All his wolf wanted to do was to make her theirs, to bite her in the same place that this other wolf, alpha or not, had dared do. "Look, miss. I'm hanging on by a thread here. If you don't want me to shift, then you must remain still. You're making him nuts."

"What is it you think you're going to do to me? Bite me too? You will not, if that's what you're thinking. And we're leaving."

Caleb held his wolf in check as long as he could. But when she threatened to leave them, he lost his hold.

Her scream was the last thing he heard as his body was consumed by his wolf.

CHAPTER 5

Sara was trying her best not to be excited. The young woman was upset, there was no doubt about that, but she was her daughter-in-law and that made Sara giddy with happiness. She handed her a pair of pants that had once belonged to Caleb, and one of his shirts. She wasn't about to cause more trouble by giving her one of her husband's, which might have fit her better.

"I'm really sorry about this. That big baboon hit me and then he...." When Quinn trailed off, Sara watched her.

Fear. Terror and a lot of other emotions flittered across her face in quick, painful looking seconds. When she reached out to touch her, give her comfort, she pulled away. Sara felt the pain of it all the way to her heart.

"I'm terrified." Sara didn't say anything, still dealing with the pain of her rejection. "When he turned like he did, all I could think about was that other man and how he had hurt me."

"He is in trouble for that. I mean, we'll find him, that's a given, but he can't go around biting humans. I mean, for all we know he had a reason for doing it, but it sounds like he did it for sport." Quinn asked her why that would matter. "Because of what has happened. You belong to.... Let me rephrase that.

You and my son are mates. You may not care about all that right now, but with Caleb, it means a great deal. An alpha bit you. A leader of a pack. And in doing so, he made it so that Caleb or any other male wolf can't touch you."

"Touch me how?" Sara wasn't sure how to start that conversation, and was glad when Quinn seemed to understand. "I don't want to have sex with him. He's an egotistical bastard, not to mention a pigheaded asshole. I'm sorry, I know he's your son, but he was really pushy when words would have been so much easier right then."

Sara had to fix this. If Quinn ran—and to her it looked as if she was going to—then Caleb would follow. And even if he didn't, if he just stayed here, he wouldn't be able to not turn into a beast, a monster that would be just as bad if not worse than the man who'd bitten Quinn in the first place.

"Do you own something that means a great deal to you? I mean, something that was your mom's? A gift from your father?" Quinn said that she had her mother's watch that she wore when Harley had been born. "All right. This watch, if I were to take it from you and have it engraved with my name on it then gave it back, what would you feel?"

"Pissed off. You've marked up something that.... Oh. I get it. But I'm not a watch. I see where you're going with this, but I don't see the connection." Sara nodded. "This guy who bit me, he didn't have sex with me. He just chased me and bit me. Caleb, I'm pretty sure that he wants to have sex. And a lot of it."

"I'm sure I don't know about the quantity of it, but yes, sex would be involved." Sara felt her face heat up. "But this man, he marked you just as I would if I were a mean spirited person who wanted to make you hurt."

Quinn got up and made her way to the window. Sara

knew that her son was out there somewhere on the land. He'd not returned when she'd asked him to, telling her that he needed to run some of his anger off. Not at the woman with her, but at himself for not having better control over himself. Sara had asked him why he was angry with himself when he'd just done what was in his nature, and he told her that he'd scared his mate badly. But the other wolf was coming in a close second with his anger too.

"I don't know what I'm supposed to do. I don't have a perfect life, but I like it. And now this man — I'm sorry again, I know he's your son — but he's pushy and bossy. He wants to come into my life and make me into something that I'm not." Sara asked her what she thought Caleb was going to make her do. "Be his sexual plaything? Be a housewife? I don't know, just knowing him the little that I do, I know he likes things his way."

"Not true. I mean, yes, he is a little persnickety about a few things. His offices for one. Caleb has an apartment in town that he's working to close up, but he never made it a home for himself. He has things, not a great deal of them, but he has a few that he is more than willing to share and let out to people. Until recently, very recently as a matter of fact, we were dirt poor yet happy. Now? Well, I don't know what we'll be other than happy." Quinn turned to her and asked her what she would do if it was her. "I would go with an open mind. I know you have one. Otherwise your business would not be as successful as it is now. Your father said that you worked the lines, worked with the people you pay to learn the jobs. So, that tells me that you're also smart. But to see you right now, I'd think that you were closed minded as well as selfish."

Sara didn't usually insult people that she didn't know.

And rarely was there a time when she felt that she had to say something to someone. But this girl was going to be her daughter-in-law hopefully, and she wanted them to start off on the right footing.

"Where is Caleb?" She told Quinn that he was more than likely out in the woods. "You can talk to him, correct? Can you please ask him to meet me by the tree line? As a person."

"I can do that." She started to point out that he'd be naked, but decided that maybe that wouldn't be a bad thing for either of them. She reached out to Caleb as she made her way down to the kitchen to finish up dinner for them all.

Why does she want me there? Sara told him she had no idea, but if she wanted to talk, he'd better listen. *Yes, ma'am, I promise you I will. Is she mad still?*

Yes. I'm not sure at who at the moment, but I'm sure that you can figure that out. He said that he'd be there as soon as he changed. *I'd not do that either if I were you. I mean.... Well, she's terrified of your wolf. Maybe you can show her that you're not like that other person and she'll trust you more.*

You think that'll help? Sara told her son that she didn't think it would hurt. *All right, but I need to get close enough to her to see who this other wolf is. Perhaps he made a mistake and thought she was his mate too.*

It didn't work that way, and she was sure that Caleb knew it. He was trying hard, as he usually was, to be diplomatic. Sara had a feeling that it was going to be a lot more than that. And when they figured out who he was, they'd be able to know why he'd done it.

"I saw Quinn go out back; you think they're going to work it out?" She told her husband that she hoped so, but they had a lot of things to work out between them. "They sure enough have a lot going against them. You know who the wolf is?"

"No, do you?" He nodded. "Kelley, is it bad? This other wolf, do we have something to worry about?"

"I'd say we do. Not just the girl, but Caleb too. It's Wade Douglas." Sara put her hand over her pounding heart. "He's not going to be happy if he meant to do this. And knowing him, I've no doubt that he did. The council, they've been after him for years, and now.... Well, if he tangles with our Caleb, it's going to be over almost afore it begins. He'll kill him."

"That won't be such a bad thing, will it?" Kelley pulled her into his arms and told her that it would be powerful bad on Caleb to take a life. "It would. I mean, he'd do it, but it would hurt him, I think. I don't know what I want to happen. To kill him would mean that it's done. But like you said, it would certainly weigh heavily on Caleb to do it."

"Yeah, I'm thinking that too. But then again, it's for his mate, so no telling." She looked up at him. "Honey, if you don't get this dinner on the table soon and stop worrying about what we can't fix right now, them boys of ours is gonna rebel. You don't wanna see that, I'm thinking."

As she got dinner put into bowls to serve, she thought about Caleb and Quinn. While Caleb was quiet, rarely speaking his mind, Quinn was the opposite. Smiling, she thought of the arguments they were going to have and how loud they'd be when she brought him out of his shell.

~~~

Quinn thought this was one of her worst ideas ever. She was walking to her doom, she thought, and worse yet, she was doing it willingly. A wolf, a big fucking wolf, said he was her mate, and there wasn't much she could do to fix it. Other than to stay away.

"Yet, here I am going to see him anyway." She stopped walking when she saw him. Quinn had no idea why she knew it was him, but when he stood up, she lifted her chin and continued on her way. There wasn't any way she was going to allow him to terrify her again.

"Your mom said she'd tell you to be a man again. If you think I'm going to let you bite me while you're like this, then you're nuts." He said nothing but did look to her right. She turned too and saw the elderly man, Mr. Winchester, coming toward her. "What's he going to do? Hold me down while you take your bite of me too?"

"Nah, I'm here to translate. His momma forgot to mention for him to shift back. Not that you'd like that any better than you do him now. He'd be in his birthday suit if'n you asked him to shift right now." Quinn looked at Caleb and then back to his dad when he laughed. "He said to tell you that he is embarrassed too."

"I'm not embarrassed." But she was. Hotly so. "Tell him that I want to talk to him. I have a lot of questions, and they're not going to get answered with him out here like this."

"I gotta tell you both something first. It's not going to go over any better than him being a wolf with you. But the wolf that bit you, I know him. Wade Douglas." She glanced at Caleb when he whimpered. "Caleb said to tell you that you're going to be safe here."

"Of course I am. I'm safe wherever I go." Mr. Winchester nodded, then shook his head. "You don't think I can take care of myself? I carry a gun, which I've been trained with, as well as hand to hand combat."

"Do you now?" She nodded. But before she could move again, Quinn found herself on her back with Caleb on her. His mouth was at her throat and his feet, paws she supposed, were holding her down. Mr. Winchester moved closer to them and knelt on one knee. "Is he hurting you?"

"No. But I want him off me now." Mr. Winchester asked her to try and do it herself. "Is he trying to make a point here? If so, I don't get it."

"Wade is an alpha. He'd be bigger than Caleb is, but not by much. And he'll have some magical power, again on account'a of him being an alpha. He can subdue you even faster than my boy here did. So, you go on and try and get him off you. He won't hurt you none."

His body was long, fitting over hers like a blanket. A blanket with teeth and claws. As she struggled to move her body out from under his or to get him off her, she thought of the other wolf, the way he had teased her. Quinn felt her fear take her breath away. Then before she could let go of the scream that she could feel building up, Caleb was over her and the wolf was gone.

"Breathe, please. Just in your nose and out your mouth. Do it slowly so you don't make yourself dizzy." She nodded, watching his eyes as he talked her down from her terror. "Keep breathing and I'll talk to you about my plans for your company."

Nodding, she watched him. There was a hint of a smile on his face, but she didn't think it was because he was making fun of her. More of a nervous one that she thought was sort of cute. But she didn't want to think of him as cute; she didn't want to think of him at all, damn it.

She was vaguely aware of Mr. Winchester leaving them as Caleb started talking. "The product that you're producing is sort of boring. Not to say that it's not good, but from the standpoint of the customer, it's pretty standard. What I would like to suggest you do is give away a one pound bag of it to ten thousand customers." She started to speak, but he cut her off again. "You're still pale, so if you don't mind, you just keep breathing and I'll keep talking. The product, like I said, is standard. Dog food. Everyone that has a dog should purchase it, if they don't just feed their dog table scraps, anyway. Even giving it a nice pretty cover, lots of air time on the television and radio, you're still selling dog food. What you need to do is get some believers."

"Hooks." Caleb nodded, and didn't tell her to keep breathing this time. "That's a great deal of cost. I mean, labeling aside, how would we market it without going in the hole before it even hits the shelves to sell?"

"A discount card. Sounds hokey, but people who love their pets love to get them things, right?" She nodded. "So stay with me here. You tell them for every ten pounds that they buy, you'll give them a punch on a card. Or something like that, I have to work on that part. But they get this punch that tells them that they have a, I don't know, a buck. Then they can cash them in on other items that you sell. Toys for the pup, coats.... I saw a woman once that had not just a coat on her puppy, but boots as well. And I'm sure that the markup on those items alone is high."

"Yes. We make a good return on those. When they sell, which we don't sell many of." She could see the idea start to bloom in her mind. "Cat food...we'd have to hit all the markets with this idea, including cats and gerbils and other pets. I don't have the cat food ready yet, but it's coming along better since the other has."

She shifted under him. He wasn't that heavy, but he was.... Quinn looked down at his chest, his very bare very furred chest, and looked up at him. He wasn't smiling, but looked like he was hurting. Shifting again, trying to figure out what was wrong with him, she saw him wince.

"You have to lie still." Nodding, she put her hand on his

rib and felt the heat of him. "You aren't lying still when you move to touch me. I'm naked and you're my mate, who is currently under me. I don't want to harm you."

"Will you? Harm me, I mean?" He shook his head. "Then what is it? Why did you threaten me with it?"

"Not harm...I shouldn't have said that. What I meant was, I don't want to strip you down and taste every single part of you." She asked him why, and felt her body warm when he growled at her. "You're not going to make this easy for me, are you? I can't touch you. You've been marked by a person that is an alpha. And in doing so, he has claimed you. I have to talk to him, see why he's done this when it's obvious that you aren't his mate. But if you keep this up, moving like this, I'm going to take you regardless of his hold on both of us."

"Maybe I'm not yours either, did you ever think about that?" He moved his head down to her throat, and she felt it all the way to her toes. His breath was warm, almost hot. Then when he licked her throat, Quinn tightened her fingers in his flesh and moaned. "What did you do to me?"

"Tasted you." It sounded so much sexier than it was. Tasting, like she was a piece of pie and he was only giving it a small little bite. But her body was heating up, her legs burned to wrap around him. And when he moved again, his hips between her thighs, she had to close her eyes when the sensations made her dizzy. "Look at me, Quinn."

"I can't. I can't.... You're making me feel too much." He said that he knew that. "Please. I want you to move from me. I don't want this. I feel like I'm going to explode."

"I'd like that, and if I move, you're going to see me." She opened her eyes and looked at him. "I'm naked, hard, and ready to plow you. If I move from you, my wolf is going to be pissy, and he'll want to take you to the ground again."

"He'll hurt me?" Caleb told her that he'd only want to mark her. "Like that other wolf, you mean? I don't want to be bitten again, Caleb. Even the one that I have now, it's not right."

"Not right how?" She didn't get the chance to answer him when he moved. "Where did he bite you? Leg? Arm? Never mind. I can smell it."

Her pants were suddenly gone. She might have been embarrassed or even pissed, but he touched his finger to the place where she'd been hurt. The scream that came from her mouth was so sudden and unexpected that she startled herself. But Caleb didn't let her go. He held her while she sobbed and screamed curses at him.

"Can you listen to me now?" She shook her head, telling him that she hated him. "Perhaps you do, but you must listen to me, Quinn. It's infected and it's seeping. You're going to be sicker, and you may die from this if we don't get you some help right now."

"It's only a little sore." He just laughed, a nervous burst of laughter that had her glaring at him. "You made it hurt by ramming your fingers into it. I wash it and keep it clean. It'll get better soon. Right?"

"No, it won't. I need for you to sit up so that I can show it to you. All right?" She didn't want to. But he was speaking to her so nicely, calmly, when she knew that he was worried. His eyes belied what his voice was saying. So, with his help, she sat up and had to cry out with the pain of it. "See the marks? Those are poison streaks. Whatever he did to you, he didn't just bite you, did he?"

"I don't know what you mean." She was getting sick now, not just with pain—and that was great—but her body wasn't feeling well. "He chased me around the parking garage, like

I said. Then when he was tired of the game, I guess, he just knocked me to the ground and did this."

"Did you bump your head? Lose consciousness at any time?" She tried to think. Had she? She shook her head, then nodded. "Quinn, you need to open your eyes and talk to me. My brothers are coming to help."

"I don't feel well." He said that he knew that and held her hand tighter. "I did hit my head, and I think I might have — but only for a few seconds — blacked out. When I was awake, I saw the blood and the tear in my stockings."

"I'm going to let you go, honey, but only for a few moments. Then I'm going to pick you up and take you to my parents' house." She was too ill to answer him, and when he laid her back on the ground, she rolled to her side and threw up.

Something warm was wrapped around her. Not even realizing that she had been cold, she tightened the blanket around her. She felt light, like a bobber at the end of a fishing line. Images sort of faded in and out. Dark and large dogs. A burning fire. Her body burned one moment, then was shivering cold the next. And she hurt, all over, including her eyelids.

Voices were loud. She knew her father's voice and Caleb's, but the rest were just blurs. She felt her clothing being stripped away, her leg touched again. But she no longer had the strength to complain. The pain now was like a throb; even to move her toes caused her sickening pain.

Quinn thought for sure she was dying. There was no way she was going to live though this; her body was closing down, and her heart hurt for her dad. She thought of her brother Harley and wondered if he'd miss her too, but that thought made her sick again, this time with worry.

"Quinn, I need you to look at me." She turned from the voice, one that she didn't know. "Quinn, my name is Daniel Hatfield. Can you hear me?"

"Hurt." He told her that he knew that, but he was going to give her something for it. The pain subsided almost as soon as he finished talking. She turned to thank him and could see that he was worried. "Am I dying?"

"Yes." She sobbed then. He nodded his head, but said that he needed to talk to her about it. "Caleb is going to change you if you'll allow it. It's risky, but it's try or you will be dead within the hour. Your body is burning up with a fever, and your organs are shutting down."

"No. He'll bite me." Daniel said it was up to her, but she would die. "No, it's just a little infection. I'll be just fine."

It was a lie, and she was sure he knew it. Her dad was there—his face blurred in and out as the drugs seemed to be making her feel better—but images were out of focus. He told her that he loved her, cried hard when she told him she was sorry. Her dad begged her once again to allow Caleb to save her. Again she told him no, that she was going to be all right.

As the drugs took her under, she could hear people talking. She wasn't sure what they were saying, but she could hear their sadness. Quinn closed her eyes when she realized that keeping them open was futile. That she couldn't see anymore. The screaming of a machine was the last thing she heard before she slipped away.

CHAPTER 6

Caleb stood in the shower and let the hot water spray over him as he stood there. His heart was broken, his body ached for what he'd had to do. He lifted his face to the showerhead and let the tears fall as he stood there. There was nothing he could do now. It was over.

She'd refused him saving her. While he could understand why, it still had hurt him that she had. But her dad had overridden her not needing help, and had begged him, literally begged him on bended knee, to save her.

"She and her brother are all I have in the world, Caleb. If you can save her, if there is the smallest chance that you can, please do it." He told him how it might very well hasten her death. "Right now, she is going to die. There is no hope for her at all."

"Mr. Dorsey, I don't think you understand what is going to—"

"I don't care what you have to do, but please, save my baby girl." Caleb had looked at his mom and dad as they stood holding one another. "Please? I'm a man who cannot live through the death of one of my children."

They knew what was going to happen and even what the outcome of this might bring to them. His dad nodded, just once, telling him that he would support him in this. Caleb had looked at his mother and she told him to do it. It was her only hope.

He'd done it with the help of not just Daniel, but his dad as well. She had screamed through the process, her body already weak with the infection. Him adding more pain to her made him hurt along with her. As he bit into her flesh, tearing it in places that he could taste what the other male had done to her, his resolve in finding him, making him pay, was compounded. Then her heart had stopped beating.

It had taken them three tries to get it going again. Daniel had never given up, for which he was forever grateful. And when she started breathing on her own, her heart beating weakly, Caleb had bitten her again, this time with so much pain in his heart that he knew that he'd never be the same again.

His mom and one of the pack women had cleaned her up of blood and other body fluids while he had gone to shift back. As he dried off, he thought of the look on Quinn's dad's face when they told him for now she was holding her own. The infection would run out now, Daniel told him, but she was far from out of the woods. Mr. Dorsey had broken down once again.

"I don't know how to thank you." Caleb said nothing. He wasn't even sure what he could say at that moment. "I know that she's going to be upset. I know that. But I'm telling you right now, you can trust me to tell you that I'll take full responsibility in that. I have my little girl back, thanks to you."

"What do you plan to tell him about the alpha?" Caleb looked at his brother Gabe when he came out of his bathroom. The thoughts that he'd been having dissipated when he spoke. "I take it no one bothered to tell him what was going to happen to you, did they?"

"No. And it won't be just me, it'll be all of us if he wants. Including Daniel and his family." Gabe nodded. "I had no choice in this, Gabe, you know that, don't you?"

"Of course I do. I'm sure I would have done the same thing had it been me." Caleb nodded, feeling at least marginally better with his support. "I've located him for you. I know that it's too late for you to ask now, but I know where he is."

Wade could and more than likely would demand payment in taking his claim. And not necessarily in the form of money, but also in lives. It mattered little that Quinn was Caleb's mate, nor would he care that she would have died without him changing her. But he'd done it now and he would have to face the consequences of his actions. So would his family.

"Are you going to tell him?" Caleb said he didn't think things would be changed if he knew or not. "I was thinking the same thing. Knowing Dorsey, the little that I do, I'd say that he'd step in where he shouldn't and get himself killed right along with us. And that's what you're expecting too, aren't you?"

"Yes. I talked to Dad about an hour ago. He said that Wade has a habit of doing this to women he finds alone. There is no rhyme or reason to his doing it either. He has no idea whether or not they're going to end up with a shifter, but he does it anyway. And if the female dies, it seems to matter little to him." Gabe asked him if he knew of any other shifter who a female had been mated to later that Wade had hurt. "Yes. Just one more. They were both killed when Wade was challenged for what he'd done. I think that the Wolf Council is looking for him for those deaths too."

"Too?" Caleb nodded as he dressed. "Caleb, I have to tell you that I've never been one to tell you what to do, but this is way beyond anything we can handle alone. Has Daniel given you the support of the pack yet?"

"Yes. He also wants me to think about taking the pack over." Gabe whistled. "Yeah, my thoughts exactly. I told him I had enough going on right now and that I can't handle much more. He said that he understood, but it might go a long way in making sure that I survived this thing with Wade."

"He's telling you to take his pack so you can kill Wade? Or is this just a temporary thing you'll be doing for him?" Caleb told him what Daniel had told him. "I see. So, he wants to work out his remaining years as a doctor for the pack instead of overseeing it. I guess I can understand that. But like you said, there is a lot going on right now. Dad doesn't know, does he?"

"No. And I'd like to keep it that way. If he found out, he'd have me taking over now." Caleb moved to the door of his room and turned back to his brother. "If I were to take over, I'd very much like for you to be my enforcer. That way if something were to happen to me, you'd be able to care for Quinn."

"You know that I will." They hugged each other and Caleb left him there. It was going to be a while before he would consider this, but if it was the only way he could save Quinn, then he'd do it.

Caleb made his way to the bedroom on the second floor. It was Dominic and Tyler's old room and had recently been painted. His mom thought that when Quinn woke, and she was positive that she would, then she'd like a fresher room. Caleb also knew that the room afforded the best view of the yard and wooded area behind the house. He sat down in the room's only other seat when his mom got up to leave.

"She's been moving a little better. I think that she'll be

waking soon. I know you can tell that her heartrate is much improved." He nodded and told her thanks. "It's my pleasure, Caleb, you know that."

"She's going to make it, I think." She nodded and smiled at him. "I might not when she finds out what I've done to her. She was very sure in her denial for me not to change her."

"She's alive, and I think that will matter to her more." His mom knew that they'd lost her several times during the process, but she didn't mention that now. "You'll see, Caleb. She'll be ever so happy that you've done this for her. Mark my words."

When he was alone with her again, he leaned back in his chair. Just as he had been doing since she'd been brought here three days ago, he watched her. And he was no closer to figuring out what he had to do with a mate than he was before. He thought about Arnold and wondered if this was his last big joke on him. That he knew that this would bring him so much confusion just to have him squirm a little.

Pulling his computer toward him again, he looked over the things he had been working on. In addition to the advertising things he had cooking for Dorsey Products, he was working on a really catchy logo and bag design for the new bakery. His mom had not only talked her friend into taking the building, but she had also been able to hire four more people to work for her. Caleb had given them a very low interest loan to have the place outfitted, and just yesterday the inspector had given the okay from the health department. Sally Anne Merchant, owner of the new bakery and sweet shop simply called The Mercantile, was as excited as he was for her new venture.

"You should try drawing on one of those tablets that has a touch screen." He looked at Quinn and waited to make sure whether she was awake or dreaming. "I think I saw one of them in your new offices."

"I have one but I've not had any time to play around with it yet. I've been slightly distracted." She nodded and rolled to her back. "How are you feeling?"

"You changed me." He nodded and put his computer down. "I know that I said that I didn't want it, but.... Where is my dad?"

"Resting. The whole house is. We've been taking turns in here with you." She looked around but didn't sit up just yet. "How are you feeling?"

"Strange. I guess that would be normal, right? To feel odd after that. I'm assuming that it went well?" He told her that there had been complications, but she was going to be all right. "Is that why I feel like I'm too weak to even move?"

"Pretty much. I don't know how much you know of a conversion from human to wolf, but it's not easy on the person. Then there was the added difficulty that you were as close to death as a person could be." She nodded and closed her eyes. He thought she was sleeping when she spoke again.

"I can see her, I think. Or it's just in my head." He told her she could more than likely see her. "She's speaking to me. Not with words, but I can tell that she doesn't want me to call her just yet. Like she knows that we're too weak for it."

"That's a good observation, and good advice too. Even though it would do you a world of good to shift, you both need to rest." She nodded and yawned, which made him do the same. "If you're hungry, I can have someone bring you up some soup. It's probably all you'll be able to handle just yet."

"Can you lay down with me?" He didn't move, thinking again that she was dreaming. "I'm feeling like I'm going to come apart, and I'd like for you to just hold me or something. Sort of center me. I know it's a lot to ask...after all, we don't know each other all that well. But I could use it."

Caleb moved to the side of the bed where she had been resting. She moved over for him, giving him more than half the bed. When he rolled to his side and wrapped his arms around her, she snuggled back against him and sighed heavily.

"I'm afraid." Caleb told her he was as well. "I guess you would be. You made me a wolf and you had no idea how I was going to take it."

"Pretty much." She nodded and settled down again. "Your father, he's going to take the blame for this, for me going against your will, but I would have done it anyway had he not asked. It was scary there for a while. You had to be resuscitated three times. But like I said, all in all, you did well."

"He begged you to do it." Caleb said nothing. "This other wolf, the one that bit me, tell me what happens now with him."

"I don't know what you mean." She turned in his arms and he looked at her. "You're still pretty weak, you should rest."

"One thing you're going to learn about me is that I don't like to be fobbed off. If I ask you something or you need to tell me about someone, please do so. I hate being in the dark about things simply because someone thinks to protect me. Tell me about this other male." She looked so determined that he smiled. "Don't be charming when I want answers, either. You'll just piss me off."

"All right, but you're not going to like it much. He's going to kill me when he finds out. You too if he can get to you. Which he won't, because the pack and my family will protect you with their lives." She asked him why they'd do that. "Because as you know, you're my mate. Even if we've never mated nor bonded, you're the one for me. And we all protect what is ours."

~~~

Quinn wasn't sure if he was serious or not, but she assumed that he was. That his family would lay down their lives for her was surreal. Not to mention insane. But for now, she'd leave it. There were other things, more information that she needed from him.

"Has he done this before? Bitten someone then left them to die?" Caleb nodded. When he ran his fingers down her arm then up again, she felt something move over her skin. Like he'd caressed her from the inside out. "What makes you think that he'll kill you and me?"

"There was a couple, a wolf and his mate. Gabe, one of my brothers, is looking into things for me…he knows a hacker that is helping him. Anyway, this alpha bit her and when her mate found her, he challenged the guy for the rights of his mate back." She asked him what that was, becoming more and more distracted every time he touched her. "I could smell him on you. Even though it had been a while since he touched you and bit you, as another wolf, I could smell it. Like a scent that says to other males to stay away, that you belong to someone else. In this other wolf's case, he knew that he couldn't touch his mate, no matter how much he wanted to, because of a more powerful scent on her. So, he found him and begged for her to be released from him. Of course he was denied, and so the man did the only thing he thought he could and fought for both their lives."

"He killed them both, didn't he?" Caleb nodded. "What sort of monster does that? I mean, he just goes around biting people, infecting them for no other reason than he can? And then when they have someone that they could fall in love with, he won't let them even have that? He's a mother fucker…you know that, don't you?"

"Yes. I've figured that out. But we don't think that he meant for you to be ill. At least that's what we're hoping. There have been other deaths associated with Wade—that's his name, by the way…Wade Douglas—but in the case of the other women, three of them committed suicide. Two more of them were killed by their mates, and one died just the way you nearly did. From an infection that no one at the human hospital could find anything to combat it with." She wanted to ask him how he'd known but didn't. She was afraid enough as it was. "We're not going to let anything happen to you, Quinn. As I said, my family and I are going to do our damnest to keep you safe. May I kiss you?"

"Yes." She had it in her head to tell him no. But before she could make her mouth work, it went ahead and decided for her. As he moved closer to her, she had a thought and stopped him with a hand on his cheek. "Will he know? This other alpha, will he know that you kissed me?"

"Christ, I hope so."

The kiss was devastating, and not in a bad way. He rolled her to her back, deepening the kiss to the point where she held him to her so that when she came apart, somehow he'd keep her there.

Her body burned for his. Not just his touch, even though she knew that he was touching her everywhere, but his very breath and soul. She wanted to feel him inside of her, touching her like no man ever had before. Quinn was sure that he would too, and would be the only man who ever would take her again. When he lifted his head, she stared into his eyes, seeing his wolf there, and hers answered whatever call he was saying to her own. It moved over her skin like it was telling her this was all right, the way things should be.

"He wants to mark you." Her first thought was no, there was no way he was going to mark her, but he moved, his body disappeared, and she was holding a wolf. *Don't be afraid of him. He'd rather die than to harm you in any way. I'd like to tell you that's all he wants, to mark you, but he wants a taste of his mate as well.*

Caleb was a voice in her head. It sounded so much like him, as if he were right there beside her, that she touched her fingers to the head of the wolf. His soft sound, almost like a purr, had her moving for him when he nudged her with his head.

His body moved over hers, not sexually, but just so that he could move to the other side of the bed. When he was settled, his big head between her legs, she felt her pussy soak, her body warm at the thought of what he might be seeing from his positon. When he moved again, crawling up the bed so that he could rest his head on her abdomen, she touched her hand to his head and petted him.

His nose moved the blanket back, his paws pulled at the sheet. When he had her exposed she sat up a little on her elbows and wondered what he was going to do now. While she waited, he moved again, burying his nose in the apex of her thighs, and Quinn nearly came.

You're driving him insane. He wants to taste your cream. So, do it. To have you come down our throats is all we can think about. Her pussy gushed, her nipples tightened when the wolf huffed at her, the heat of his breath against her panties making her closer to the edge than she'd ever been before. *We want you, need you to come for us. Release, Quinn, do it so he can have his fill.*

Her panties were gone when the big wolf took the elastic in his teeth and pulled them away. The lacey garment hung in his mouth for several seconds, and all she could think about was that he'd stripped her. Quinn spread her legs for him then, opening her thighs so that they could both smell her.

The tongue that lapped at her was rough and long. She wanted more, needed it all, and he gave it to her. With each stroke of his tongue, every time he touched her clit, she cried out. And then when he entered her with his rough tongue, Quinn came hard enough to make her body ache for more.

Caleb was suddenly there, his hands on either side of her hips, his mouth poised over the most sensitive part of her. And when he suckled her clit into his mouth and bit down, she screamed again. Nothing on this earth could have prepared her for the shattering of every thought she'd ever had about sex. This was so much bigger, so much better it made her head spin.

Her body was twisted up with every climax; each release brought her closer to something that she knew was going to be epic. Caleb ate her, feasted on her no matter how many times she begged him to stop, that it was too much. Then when he lifted his head finally, he crawled up her body, nipping at her as he went.

He took her nipple in his mouth and chewed on it none too gently. She was writhing beneath him, her body needing whatever he had promised without words to give to her. As his cock slipped into her pussy, just enough to know that he was going to fill her, he was going to hurt her, she knew. Then he kissed her.

His cock moved in and out of her over and over, touching her clit, bringing her painfully closer to the edge again. Wrapping her legs around his, she moved with him stroke for stroke, trying to get him to fill her completely. Then when he slammed forward, his cock feeling like it was tearing her apart, she screamed again, this time in pain.

Caleb was speaking to her as he held her. He hadn't moved since he'd taken her, but held her in his arms like a man would a wounded bird. The words that he was saying were unclear, but their meaning, his intent to calm her, was very clear.

"I'm sorry. I wanted to make it quick, never thinking that I'd hurt you more." Quinn shifted her hips, trying to dislodge him, when he put his hand on her hip and stilled her. "You have to be still. I think I've said this to you before and you just don't do it."

The humor in his voice made her smile. And when he lifted his head from her neck where he'd been, she could see so much there that she'd not noticed before. A scar on his forehead, a small indentation on his cheek. There was also a mark on his lip, one on his earlobe that made her think he'd had it pierced before. But what she saw in his eyes was compassion, understanding, and happiness.

"You are very large." He thanked her. "Not meant to be a compliment right now. I should have told you I'd never had sex before."

"I knew it. The first time I saw you, I could smell it." She moved again and he groaned. "Is this your payback for me being so large?"

She rolled her hips, feeling him there inside of her as she tightened around him. His breaths were hot, his mouth so close to hers. Pulling him to her, she kissed him as she moved again.

He took her gently. His body was large, his cock thick, but he didn't hurt her again. Instead he gave her the most incredible pleasure, several times. And when he told her to come with him, his body pounding hers just a little harder, she came at the same time, her body bowing up off the bed in a way that brought his throat near her mouth. Not thinking about what she was doing, Quinn bit him there, licked along the path of his large vein and bit down hard on the pulse when she found it with her tongue.

That set off a climax so hard, so fulfilling that she knew that it was what she'd been waiting for. What she'd been born to have. And when she came a second, then third time, she held him to her as he came again and again, shouting out his release as loudly as she was.

Her last thought was that he was going to kill her with sex. His body was going to wear her to the very bone, and she couldn't find a thing wrong with that.

CHAPTER 7

Wade saw the woman moving between the cars. Like that was going to save her from him, he thought. He'd been doing this a great deal longer than she had been out of diapers. As he moved closer, forever keeping his eyes on her, a touch of something foreign touched his mind. Not really a voice but something.... A bitch, his bitch, had been taken.

Pausing in his pursuit of the woman, he laid down. He had to think, had to remember which of them he was going to have to kill along with the male. Wade didn't care that they lived, but he had marked them for a reason, and they'd fucking better remember that or he'd have to teach them a lesson.

He made it a point to make sure that he took just enough blood of the bitches to make sure that he could keep tabs on them. The problem was, he wasn't ever sure who was who. He supposed it was a case of just too many, but he knew that he'd figure it out soon enough. Laughing a little, he moved under the car next to the one that had the scent of the bitch he was going to mark next and waited. This one would be along soon enough, then he could go and find the one that was going to pay for taking a mate without his permission.

Not that he ever gave it. This was a game to him, one that

he enjoyed more than he did sex. And Wade was the best there was at fucking. He knew this because all the pussies that he fucked never complained. Of course, they were dead, but that wasn't the point.

He heard the remote beeping of the lock on the car next to him and hunkered down to attack. This was going to be too easy, but he thought that it might be fun to mark a bitch during the busiest part of the day, after work. Just as he was ready to make his move, he heard a voice.

"You shouldn't be out here alone, April. There are all kinds of monsters around now. Did you read about that women that was attacked by a dog the other night?" He most certainly wasn't a dog, but he liked that people were talking about him. "I'll wait until you get in your car, then I'll go too."

"Well, aren't you the sweetest thing. Thank you, Frank." Yeah, thanks Frank, Wade thought. You've fucked up my fun. "Why don't we go and get a drink after work tomorrow night? I don't know about you, but this has been the week from hell. I'm glad that Caleb got out on his own. But it sure has made David a real prick."

They talked for several more boring moments. Wade had already decided to kill the fucking Frank, but he had to wait for the bitch to leave. He'd be back to get her, but it would have to wait now. Wade liked the excitement of it being busy, but he wasn't stupid enough to think he'd get out without some injury with someone right there with him.

When the woman was gone, her car spraying exhaust in his face, Wade watched the feet of the man. He'd follow him to the ends of the earth to kill him, but he just stood there. Finally, just as he was ready to pounce, the man spoke again.

"You best be on your way." He wondered who he was talking to when he went down on bended knee and looked right where he was. "I know you're there. I can smell you. Wolf. And if I don't miss my bet, I'm thinking you might be the one biting those women."

Wade knew that with his dark fur he was well hidden. But if the man was telling the truth, then he already knew where he was as well as had his scent. That was dangerous to him, especially if this man wasn't human. When he heard the click of something, Wade looked up again to see that the man had a gun pointed at him.

"You move toward anyone in this parking garage again, and I will hunt you down and fill you full of silver. You hear me? This is a public parking garage, but I know your scent now and you're so fucked if I get even a whiff of you being around here." Wade wanted to leap at his throat and tear it out. But he knew as surely as he was cowering here, that the man would do just as he said. "I'm going to stand up now and let you go. But mark my words, you come here again and it will be over for you. They'll find your naked assed body full of holes if I smell you around here again."

True to his word, the man stood up and backed away. Wade wanted to get his scent, sort of return the favor of threatening him too, but the man was ready for that. He stood there, his gun pointed right at him, as he made his way out from under the car. Wade was nearly to the woods behind the garage when he wondered about something. If he'd knew he was the one biting the bitches, why didn't he kill him?

"He's a pussy, that's why." Wade went to his hiding place and shifted. Turning in the mirror, he looked himself over. He never wanted to be killed as a wolf. Not that he thought anyone would actually kill him, but he didn't want that to ever be an option. To be found dead was bad enough, but to be buck assed naked would be just too much.

His body wasn't what it used to be, he knew this, but he was in pretty good shape for a man his age. Laughing, he decided that his logic was off but he was happy with it. Dressing, he thought of the man, the one that had threatened him.

There was a lot of things the person could have been. Another wolf wouldn't have done anything but allowed him to do what he wanted. As a former alpha, Wade knew that he still had the scent of one, as well as the strength. But what he didn't have was the pack, nor the sanction of the council. They had given him the boot long ago.

Wade was nearing his seventieth birthday, and knew that most wolves would have been retired and enjoying their golden years. He'd never wanted that, never wanted to be sitting back on a porch swing watching younger and stupider wolves run around fucking up his world. And women....

He had nothing against women. He liked them for the most part. Wade knew that he had no respect for them, but that didn't mean they didn't have their uses. It was just the way he was. He disliked human women more than he did anything. However, that wasn't the reason that he bit them, sometimes killing them. It was because he wanted no competition in this world if they were to birth a brat by another shifter. He didn't care if a human found them and had brats, but a wolf would know better. Or he'd better anyway.

He figured that if he bit every single woman that he encountered, he'd eventually weed out the stronger ones. Another alpha's bitch. A kid born of them that would come along and try to take him out. He'd come up with this idea about five years ago, when a brat of about seventeen had decided to challenge him for his territory. And he'd won.

Wade had left in shame, his tail literally between his legs

as he made his way shamefully out of the area. He'd not even gone back for his family, his wife and two daughters, but had hidden in a cave and healed. By the time he was strong enough to go back, not only were they dead, but his house had been taken over by the upstart and his own family. Wade had moved on, deciding that someday he'd be back for the prick.

His wife had been a disappointment to him anyway. No matter how many times he'd filled her belly with his seed, she'd only had the two babies. And both were girls. He wanted a son, one that could have taken over his pack when he was ready to retire. So, in a way, the kid that had challenged him had done him a huge favor. He didn't have to think about his family any longer.

Dressing in his suit, he made his way to his car. There were some things, like traveling in a lovely car, that he missed about having his own pack. This piece of shit that he had now had bald tires, an engine that missed cylinders on occasion, and a radio and heater that no longer worked. When he finally got it started, it took several tries for it to go in a forward motion. Wade knew that he was going to have to do something about replacing it very soon, or he'd be back to walking everywhere.

The bitch. He tried to sort through his memory of scents and actions to find the one that had dared defy him. There were three that he could pinpoint, and one of them had been in the same building that he worked in. He was sure that it wasn't her…he thought that she'd died. Stupid cunt. It had to be one of the other two. And as soon as he got to work, he was going to do a little search on them.

Wade waved at the two men at the front desk when he entered the building. He wanted their jobs. Being a cop, it was about all he'd ever hoped for as a person. But age now played a huge factor in the kind of jobs that he could do. And being a mailman for them was about as close as he figured he'd ever get now that he was supposed to be retiring. Working here, in the station with other cops, had given him a great deal of information.

"Hey Doug, I was wondering if you'd look something up in the mail room for me. I was expecting this package to come to me last week, and they're saying that it was delivered here." Wade smiled and said that he'd do it. "Thanks, man. You're the best. I'll check back in with you later to see what you could find."

Wade made his way back to the check-in area. These people were supposed to be the finest, and they had no idea that a man that they were looking for was right under their noses. His fictitious name was just a play on his own. Wade Michael Douglas had slipped right in as Doug Michael about six or seven years ago with a name he'd been using for a long time when he wanted to do an odd job or two.

He'd done it for the money at first. Then later so he could claim to anyone who asked that he worked for the police department. But he soon realized that he could use it to his advantage. Wade had gotten good at misdirecting their investigation into the canine bitings around town. And he'd also figured out that he could slip in and out of the evidence room without setting off the monitors if he just acted his age a little. A fumbling old man could get by with a great deal, he'd come to know.

Then there was the evidence storage itself. He'd been able to get out some pretty nice shit. Not that he felt he needed it, but fencing it had gotten him some ready cash. Not a lot; he was careful not to take too much, but enough to supplement his daily living expenses. But he figured it was there for the taking, and why not make a little cash?

The delivery was right where it should have been. Taking it up to his desk, he set it aside while he logged into the departmental files. He wasn't sure of names for the women, but that was easily solved when he brought up the case files. But he was confused as to why there were only two when he knew that there were three in this area. As he continued to track down the ones that he could find, he made notes on where the bitches lived and worked.

"You found it." He nodded, making sure not to look as irate as he felt for being interrupted. "Anything I can do for you, just let me know. I was worried that the missus would have found this thing, and it's for her birthday next week."

Wade wanted to point out that she'd have no way of finding it since he hadn't, but didn't comment. Instead he asked him about the third woman. In a sly, roundabout way, by asking about the other two.

"It says here that one of them was in the hospital. Do you know if she was released or not?" The cop looked over his shoulder and Wade had to calm his beast. The nerve of some people, getting into his space. "I see that there were two of them. I was wondering how far along we were in their claims."

"Sort of been put on the back burner, I guess. I was there for the second victim. It was uncanny how her story matched the other ones. But Missy Winds, she killed herself. I don't know the details about her death, but I'm sure that it's in here. The other woman? Don't know. I can find out for you. Better yet, here. Let me give you my log in so you can search." As he wrote down the information Wade thought that he was the stupidest man alive. Who gave out their log in and password like this? "I don't usually do this sort of thing, so by the end of the day it'll be changed. So do what you have to do in a hurry.

I can't let that get out. Not that I don't trust you, but you know how the department can be about sharing shit like that."

After logging in, Wade glanced up at the clock. He had less than six hours to get as much information as he wanted. And not only that, but with this guy's log in, no one would realize it was him searching. He liked that a great deal. It wasn't until he'd been at it for over an hour that Wade discovered that he had tristate access. He could dip into the data base of the surrounding states, ones he'd been to and bitten bitches, and see where they were. Wade was going to enjoy this.

~~~

Caleb wasn't sure what he wanted in a house, but he was reasonably sure that this wasn't it. The house was older, had a lot of space, but it felt like a cave. There was only one bathroom per floor, and the closet in the master bedroom was smaller than the one in the apartment he'd had. He looked at Quinn when she joined him in the kitchen. She didn't look any happier about this one than he was.

"It's old." He nodded and said he could see that. "I'm betting that it'll take a lot of work to get it up to even standard working order. I mean, the bathroom on this floor has a pull chain to flush."

"And the mudroom off the kitchen is falling in. I think we can do better than this one, don't you?" She was still shy about buying a house with him. Not that he blamed her. They were new to everything they did together. "There are four more houses on our list. I'm thinking this one should be marked off. What about you?"

"Oh yes." They made their way out to his car. It was new too. Something he'd never had before was a new car and he'd picked out a little sports number, but decided that since he had a family, although only a small one at the moment, a bigger car with four wheel drive would be better suited to them. "Can I look at the list? I mean, I know that you are more familiar with the area, but I can read off what it has while you drive."

"Sure." He gave her the list and started the car. "So you know, the ones on that list aren't all that is in the area. I just wanted something close to my family. My parents are the world to me."

"I can understand that. They're very nice people." She started reading over the list to him. None of the ones on his list appealed to him anymore. Caleb wanted a home, not a place to sleep. He started to tell her to just toss it out, they'd start all over, when she spoke again, her voice breathless. "Caleb, slow down. Look."

He saw the For Sale sign when she pointed it out to him. From the rode the house wasn't visible, so he turned down the gated drive and stopped. He thought they'd found their new home.

The drive wasn't long, but he loved the way that it curved around in front of the big house. There were four shuttered windows on the top floor and the same on the bottom, with a curved front porch and a double front door. On either side of the house were wings that were set back several feet, each with two windows at the top, as well as huge picture windows on the lower level on each side. He could see a screened in area that was off to the side of the house and a couple sitting in it. Caleb drove up to the house when they came out of the area.

"Well, howdy there." He nodded at the elderly gentlemen and shook his hand when it was offered. The woman he introduced first as his wife. "This is my lovely bride, Rae. I'm Cliff. We're the Grahams. You lost?"

"No, house hunting as a matter of fact. This is my future

wife, Quinn Dorsey, and I'm Caleb Winchester. We saw your sign and decided to have a look." The man grinned, his face nearly splitting open with it. "It's a beautiful place."

"Thank you. My wife and I, we've raised up our children here for about forty years. But it's a mite too big...did you say Winchester? Your daddy Kelley Winchester?" He nodded, wondering what his father had done now. "Well I'll be dog waddled. You're the Winchester boy that helped out old man Cartwright, aren't you?"

"I am." Mr. Graham told him he was sorry for his loss. "He was a good man. One that I miss more and more daily."

"Yes, sir. He was a good man. And a good friend to all that knew him." He looked at the house then back at the two of them. "Well, come on in and have yourself a looksee. So you know, we're willing to part with all the furniture too. We've got us a nice little condo in town that's all on one floor. You two go on in and me and the missus, we'll be right there in the sun room when you're a mind to come find us."

He was shy about just going through the house, but Quinn took his hand and led the way. As soon as they entered the big antebellum of a house, he knew that he wanted to raise his own cubs in this house and have his family come visit too. The grand entrance hall was big enough to serve dinner to his family. And as they made their way through the nine bedrooms and baths, the master suite that had a large patio that led out onto a swimming pool and bath house, Caleb was trying to think about how much it would cost to not just heat the place, but to keep it cool in the summer months.

"It's grand, isn't it?" He nodded. The kitchen they were in would make any chef drool over it. "There is so much room to move around in. And all the rooms are so open and lovely. The master suite, I could almost stay in it for the rest of my days."

"The office, did you see that? I could get so much work done in there that I'd not want to go to the office in town at all. And it's within walking distance of everything." She nodded and sat on the stool that sat near a large butcher block. "You want this, don't you? I mean, I do as well, but could you see yourself living here for the rest of your life?"

"I could. With the right husband." He nodded, then got down on one knee before her. "I was joking, Caleb. You don't have to pretend to marry me."

"I'm not. Pretending I mean. I want to marry you. Actually, I think I need to." He pulled out the little blue box. It had been a chance, he knew, to propose to her. They'd only known one another for about a week now, but he did love her. So did his wolf. "I started to ask your dad to help me out with this, but I wanted to scout it out first. This ring, it sort of called to me. It's perfect for you."

The ring was a wide band with a dark blue diamond as the setting. The band, which was what he'd fallen in love with first, was a creation of art. A forest of trees was etched along it, and just in the tree line was a wolf. The jeweler said he thought it was a dog, but Caleb knew better.

"I've said my whole life that I have no desire to marry. I had good reasons...at least I thought they were. I was mostly concerned about money and supporting a family. But then... well, you came along and changed my mind." She asked him the real reason that he was asking her today. "That's a good question and one that I'll answer you truthfully. I'm not sure you'll believe me or not, but I'm in love with you."

He knew that she didn't believe him. Caleb was having a hard time with it too. Who knew that being in love with someone could be so all consuming? But in a good way. He

109

slipped the ring on her finger when she didn't say anything. Kissing her hand, he turned it over to the palm and traced the long line there.

"When you were dying, all I could think about was that I'd have nothing if you were to pass. Nothing. And even though I'd only just met you, it was as if you centered my life. Put me together and on the right path." He looked up at her then. "The first time that you coded, I felt as if my life had ended with yours. And every time, each and every time they were able to bring you back to me, I swore to myself that I would make you the center of my world too, and do everything in my power to keep you safe."

"You are the most romantic man I've ever had the pleasure of being in love with." He stood then, pulling her into his arms as she told him she'd gladly marry him. "Now. Let's see how much they want for this house and the contents, and move in."

The Graham's were just where they had first seen them. Mr. Graham was having a glass of tea; the missus was having a cup of it. They were laughing when they entered the sun room, and both stood up when they saw them. Caleb had a sudden thought of a movie he'd seen long ago about a big house and an elderly woman. He hoped they weren't getting themselves a money pit.

"Well, son? What do you think? Think you can bring up some babies here? Make them a nice home?" Caleb said that he thought he could. "I know your daddy would love to see you this close. I heard you boys were remodeling their home. That's a nice thing to do for them."

"We tried to get them to move into something newer, but Mom said she has roots there deeper than an oak and she wasn't leaving. Dad said the same. He said the farm needs him." Mr. Graham nodded. "About this house...."

"We've been talking it over, me and the missus, and we decided that we want you to have it. Not that we've not had a few offers, but well...they didn't seem the kind of people that would fill this house with love and laughter." Caleb squeezed Quinn's hand and Mr. Graham commented on it. "People don't do that much anymore. Hold hands. It's like they got too much going on in them to realize what's right there with them. Filling up their hands and heads with stuff that don't mean squat at the end of the day. So, you two make us an offer and we'll go from there."

"I wouldn't even begin to know where to start with an offer, Mr. Graham. You tell us what you're asking for it and we'll think about it." He told them a figure. Caleb looked at Quinn then back at him. "That's really low, don't you think? I mean, I'd love to take it off your hands for that, but I think you're taking a major loss on it."

"No. If you agree, then we're all for it. Includes the furniture too. We want you to take it off our hands and fill it for us. Children need to be here, and love."

Caleb wasn't sure what to say. The asking price for just the house was well under market value, he knew. But to include the —

"We'll take it on one condition." Mr. Graham asked Quinn what that would be. "You'll spend every holiday you can here with us. Help us fill the house with that love. You know the Winchester family...well, I'd like for you to get to know mine as well. Will you do that for us?"

He looked over at his wife. Mrs. Graham had tears in her eyes and got up to hold her husband's hand. At her nod, Mr. Graham turned to them and nodded as well.

"It's be our pleasure. Yes, ma'am, I think we're getting

the best deal all around for our old house. And you didn't ask, but I'll tell you, ain't a thing wrong with it. This house has been gone over top to bottom every year. You're going to love living here." Caleb told him he thought they just might. "Good to hear. Yes, that's wonderful to hear."

CHAPTER 8

Kelley was sitting on the porch, just having a nice relaxing time of it, when the car pulled into his drive. He didn't know the car, but made no effort to get up and see who it was. And when the big man got out of it, he continued to sit there but reached for his sons.

I got me a fancy dressed man standing in my yard. He's got on a suit and carrying one of them manly purses. Xander asked if it was a purse or a briefcase. *Same difference if you ask me. But I guess you younger kids would call it a briefcase. Can you come on around here? I'd surely hate to have nary a witness when I have to take him out.*

Dad, please don't kill him. For all you know, he could have one of those big checks for you. Kelley told Gabe that he didn't see one, but he'd hold judgment for now. *Thank you. I think. I'm with Owen and Tyler, and we'll be there in five minutes.*

I'm with Quinn, and we're turning up the drive now. I can see Dominic and Xander too. Kelley felt better just knowing that they were coming. Not that the man had done anything untoward yet, but he wasn't going to take any chances. When his Sara came out to join him, the man was just stepping up on the porch.

"Hot day, isn't it?" Kelley just nodded, saying nothing.

He knew that the boy was a cat, tiger, and he wasn't one of the wimpy ones either. Kelley thought he might be the pack leader to his group. "I'm sorry to barge in on you unannounced, but there doesn't seem to be a listing for the house here."

"No, there'd not be." The man looked confused but didn't comment. "You came a long way off the road there, fella. You need directions?"

Caleb and Quinn pulled in then. Both of them got out of the car and walked up on the deck. Caleb was a mite bigger than the stranger, but it didn't seem to bother him overly much. Quinn asked him his name.

"Oh, sorry. Jamie Patterson…no relation to the author, if you were gonna ask." Kelley didn't read anything but the paper, but he figured out there someplace was an author with that name. "I'm a cop, actually. I have…. Well, I'm not sure if it is anything or not, but I wanted to let you know something that happened at the precinct where I work."

He opened his manly purse and handed him a file just as the rest of his boys pulled in the drive. When he grinned at him, Kelley had a feeling that the man thought him a little off to call in so many when he was just a person, but Kelley didn't take chances with his family.

"Hello, Jamie. I didn't miss lunch with you, did I?" Xander looked over at him. "Dad, this is my friend at the station. He's the guy that has been helping me with permits and all."

"Why the heck didn't you tell me you were a friend of one of my boys? Scared the bejebbes out of me. I had to go calling them in when I'm sure they had things to do." Kelley wasn't mad, not really, but he had been scared for his wife. She was all he had in the world except for his boys, and he'd not have some fool hurting her. "I tell you, I ain't never."

None of them asked him what he wasn't ever going to do.

It was just something he said. Kelley had been trying to break the habit of saying it, but he was too old to change his path now, he thought. Instead, he invited the man into the house for some tea.

"Thank you, yes. Xander was telling me about a wolf that might be around asking questions. He works at the station where I do. Well, he doesn't work so much as complains a great deal. I always knew that he was a wolf…never really thought much about it, to be honest. He's an elderly man, keeps up with himself and gets around all right. We judged him to be in his seventies or so. We never worked together…I work nights and weekends, he usually works days, like I said, handing out mail and running errands. Then yesterday, Bill, another cop who is stupider than a rock, gives him his log in." Kelley asked what sort of log in. "To get into the systems. You see, Bill has a pretty high clearance because he works on high profile cases. When Bill mentioned to me that he had to remember to change his password, I asked him what he'd done. Imagine my surprise when he told me that he'd given it to old Doug to do some searches. I went to see what he had been looking at later."

Kelley handed the file over to Caleb and he shared it with the boys. Kelley might have been able to figure out what it said, but he was more interested in what this man had to say. And from the looks on the boys' faces, there was going to be plenty. And nary a bit of it good news.

"After finding out that he'd been looking into some unsolved cases about the women who have been attacked, I thought he might be related to one of them. But after doing a search on his name, I came up with nothing. And his social that we have on file, it's to a dead man that passed about twenty some years ago." Another sheet of paper was handed

115

out, but just to his sons. "I started playing out with his name. Just trying different ways it might be put together, then shortened forms of it. That's when I realized that his name isn't Doug Michael at all, but Wade Michael Douglas. And he's been in trouble with the law for some time. That's when I remembered the name that Xander asked me to keep an eye out for."

"Holee Christmas trees. He's here, right here in town?" Bill nodded and said he was sorry he'd not figured it out earlier. "And why would you know that was him? He's been slipping around the radar for a long time now, and you did good in catching him when nobody else could. You done us a good thing, coming out here and letting us know. He's not a good man. Hurt my daughter-in-law there too."

"I'm sorry about that as well, but you're right, he's not a good man. I have Wade's record with me for you to see. He has a list that is as long as this table on things that he's been attached to, but only things that we're aware of. Three months ago, he was a person of interest in the death of two elderly women. We think now that they might have come up on him when he was hurting a younger woman. Three days after their bodies were found, the young woman came in to file a complaint that she'd been bitten by a dog. The station is out looking for a dog, not a wolf. But as you can well imagine, I've kept that part to myself so that they don't go on a shooting rampage."

"And there ain't no way for us to make them change their mind, either. And if'n we did, like you said, every wolf around would be killed for them just being what they were." Jamie said that nothing on four legs would be safe. "No, I guess you got that right too."

"Xander told me that his sister-in-law was bitten. I'm

assuming that would be you, miss?" Quinn said he'd attacked her in a parking garage. "Yes, that would be his way. In addition to the ten or so women that we know of, I believe that there are others, ones that never reported it. We have no way of knowing of course, but that's just what I think."

"So what do you suggest we do now? We can't just let him keep doing what he's doing now that we know who he is and where. I mean, there are a lot of women out there that can be hurt by this turd." Kelley felt his face heat up at the usage of that word. He knew there were worse curse words out there, but he never used them. "He's an alpha. Or he was at one time. Don't think he'd have himself a pack, do you?"

Caleb said he doubted it. "But then, he might have himself a small one, a few renegades like himself that does this for the pure joy of it. Or to get back at someone. I don't think so however. If there was a pack that did what he did, I'm pretty sure we'd be dealing with a lot more women than we are at present."

Jamie cleared his throat before speaking. "As I said, he works at that station. Not on cases or anything, but he's there with some access. He could very well have been looking for addresses to go and pay these women a visit."

"You mean me." It took Kelley a few seconds to realize what Quinn was getting at. "He'd know then, that I've taken a mate? Will he also know that I've been converted?"

"No. Once you and my boy there came together, his...I guess you could call it his attachment to you was severed. Don't mean he can't find you, not with him taking a bite of you. But he can't make you do anything you don't wanna. Not that I think he coulda anyway, but usually, that's the way it would work." Quinn asked him what that meant. "Well, he could make you do things with him. You know...he could

117

control you, make you do stuff you'd not normally do. Like... well, he could make you jump off a building or something. As it is now though, he can do just about anything he wants in form of a repayment."

"Such as?" He didn't want to tell her. Kelley hated to have brought it up even, but his tongue got ahead of his head again. "You mean he could kill him. You're saying that his form of payment would be to kill Caleb for something that he did to me."

"Yes. He could kill us all." Kelley wanted to smack Caleb in the back of the head when he told her that. But before he could act on it, he spoke again. "I told you I'd never lie to you. Well, this is the truth. He could kill us all for what he could consider harboring you. And anyone else that he deems a threat to his marking you."

"Then I should go. Leave before he figures out I'm here." Caleb said it was much too late for that. "What do you mean?"

"If you leave, I'm going with you. And in doing that, I won't have the help of my family to protect you. And he would know who your mate is simply by smelling you. He'd also know that you were a wolf. It would only be a matter of time before he took you and raped you. It would be the only way that he could remark you. Then because he could, he'd kill you while I watched or vice versa, and then my family." Poor Quinn shivered and Caleb pulled her into his arms. "I love you, Quinn, and I'm going to do everything in my power to keep you safe."

"That goes for me too." Kelley was never so proud of his Xander than he was at that moment. But when the other four did the same, he could have about busted. "But we have to have a plan. Without one, he could simply take you. I think we should take him out first."

~~~

Caleb drove them back to his little apartment. They were set to move into the new house in a few days, after the Grahams got their end of the paperwork finished up. Caleb had wanted to pay cash for the house, but they cautioned him on that, telling him that he needed a mortgage to establish himself some credit. So, he'd called the bank, told them what he wanted, and within ten minutes after he hung up, not only did the bank manager come to sign off on the deal, but he had a check for the house made out to the Grahams.

"I was wondering something about this other person. You told me he was an alpha. How does a wolf become one of those? I mean, it's not as easy as just saying that you are, is it?" He told her that it was a lot harder than that. "Like how? I mean, I really want to know."

"You can be born an alpha. There are a lot of wolves out there that are descendants of great leaders that don't have a pack of their own. A long time ago, like decades, when an alpha was taken out, killed for his position, his family was killed as well. I don't think that happens so much anymore, but it used to happen a great deal. Our kind did this to ensure that the strongest were in the position to protect those that he cared for. The family was killed, mostly so that their descendants wouldn't come back for revenge, and also because an alpha would have children that were strong too and may challenge the alpha for the position again." Quinn asked if this went on today. "Yes. Not so much anymore, but I'm sure that there are a lot of packs led by older wolves that stick to the old laws because they work to their advantage. Daniel isn't like that. I think, along with a few other archaic laws, that one has been removed from the laws."

"Sounds very barbaric. And these packs, they're made up

119

of like thinking wolves, correct?" He told her not necessarily. "I don't understand this at all."

"A pack leader, an alpha, rules a region. It would depend, I guess, on how many pack he had to determine the size of his territory. Our alpha is Daniel…you've met him. He wants to retire soon, and since he has no sons to pass it down to, which he could, then he can pick someone to take his pack from him. That doesn't mean there won't be someone out there that wants to challenge this new alpha, but that's how that works." She asked him if he would take it if asked. "I was asked. A few days ago. Daniel said that he thought I'd make a great leader, but I turned him down."

"Why? You'd be great at it. People already come to you for advice and such." He told her it wasn't the same. "Then explain it."

"We would both run the pack. Make sure that there is enough food and housing for them all. We'd have to be there for disputes, large or small. As a pack, we rule, which means that we would enforce rules, give out punishments, and take care that they're safe." He pulled into the parking space that had been his since he moved in. Caleb turned to look at her. "To be honest with you, I've never thought of running my own pack. I was just glad to be able to make it from day to day and have a little fun."

"But you've changed your mind, haven't you?" He nodded, but then shook his head. "That's my man, as decisive as ever. What makes you think you can't do this? I'm assuming that's what's holding you back from being an alpha. Or is it that you weren't born to be one?"

"I'm the oldest son to an alpha." He knew that he had shocked her, but it was all right. He'd been feeling that way since his dad had told him a few hours ago about their family history. "My grandfather was an alpha, his dad was one, and on back for a few generations. But dad felt, with the money problems that my family has had for some time, it was better left for a man that could make sure that the pack had resources. And time. With Dad having six sons, a farm, and a job, he told me that it was an easy decision for him to step down and turn it over to a person who could do a better job."

"Your dad is a very admirable man." Caleb thanked her and told her he thought so as well. "But this thing with this other alpha, this Wade guy...if you're an alpha, do you, I don't know, sort of trump him?"

"I'm not sure what you mean." She said she wasn't sure either. "Do you mean that I would be stronger than him? If so, I haven't any idea. I think time will tell on that one. But I do know that certain things, such as power and strength, do come into being alpha. I'd have the backing of the pack. I have that now, but I'd have more control over what happens when I confront him. Also, the council, the Wolf Council, would help me faster than they would if I wasn't alpha."

"You mean when he challenges you for me. Are you sure that he'll even bother? I mean, we aren't doing anything to him now." Caleb thought of the best way to tell her, tell her that it would matter little to Wade. And their happiness might be the one thing that would make him want to kill them both. "Caleb, tell me."

"He'll not be happy that we're in love. In fact, I would imagine that he'd get more pleasure from taking the pack if he knew. But he'd feel, I think, that you've betrayed him in some way. He's a sick individual if you haven't gotten that yet." She nodded and asked him what else. "If I get challenged and I lose, then he'll take the pack. All of it. And he could make them into himself. Even if they didn't want to, they'd have to because he ruled them."

"You mean he'd make them all into monsters." Nodding, he told her that those that went against him would die. "He's a real bastard, you know that? Okay, so what we need to do is get you as alpha and then train you not to get killed. I know you can do it, Caleb. You just have to believe that you can. Because as much as I like being a wolf, I don't want to be a slave to this prick. He's going to have to die."

They went into his little place. Caleb looked at it with fresh eyes. It never really mattered to him what it had looked like before, other than clean, but now he was seeing how shabby it looked. He told her how sorry he was.

"Don't be. It has a bed, and right now that's all that matters to me. I'm exhausted." He felt the disappointment all the way to his heels. Her laughter made him pout more just to be funny. "I'm not that tired. I was hoping you might have a way to make me relax a little. I don't suppose you have any, I don't know... sexual tools, do you?"

"Oh, I do. A lot of relaxation tools, as a matter of fact. And if you let me have my way, I'll teach you how to relax me too." She pulled him to his bedroom, and he decided that as soon as they moved, he was getting a much bigger bed. The one in the house had a full, and he wanted a super king to play on. "I'm going to strip you down, slowly. And you're going to be a good girl and let me."

"I am? I don't know about that. You've opened the door to me loving sex with you, and I like to touch you." He felt his cock shift in his pants and had to adjust himself or be in pain. She eyed his cock and he felt it grow tighter. "I think you need help with that."

Before he could guess her intentions, she dropped to her knees in front of him. As she unsnapped his pants and lowered the zipper, all he could think about was how much he loved her. Then she freed him and he felt empowered by her touch.

"I've never done this before. So, if I mess up, you'll let me know?" He nodded, incapable of speech right then. She looked like a goddess, and he loved her. "The thought of taking you in my mouth, it has me soaking wet."

"Christ, woman. You're killing me." She licked his thick crown and he reached out to hold onto something. The dresser behind him moved when he grabbed it. "Quinn, you're going to make me come all over you if you don't do something.... Mother fuck."

Her mouth was hot, her tongue talented. When she curled her tongue around his cock, Caleb gripped the dresser so tightly that he was sure it would have marks in it. Then she moved, bobbed her head up and down on his shaft until he thought he was going to die.

Caleb was so close to coming when she cupped his balls that he saw stars behind his closed eyes. Wrapping his hand into her hair, he was going to pull her away, make her stop before it was too late, when she gave them a little squeeze. There was no hope for it. He let out a cry of pleasure as his balls emptied down her throat.

He was breathing hard when she pulled from him. There was a little cum on her lip and as he watched her, she licked it off and grinned at him. Caleb leaned over and picked her up from the floor as he made his way to the bed. But the wall was closer, and perfect for what he had in mind. So lifting her so that he could take her breast through her clothing, he pressed her against the wall.

"Fuck me." Gladly, his mind screamed at him. "Hurry, Caleb. I need to feel you inside of me."

He tore at her clothing, and the sound of it tearing from

her excited him more. When she was naked, he pulled her to his cock and slammed forward, taking both their breaths away. Pausing, he looked into her lust filled eyes.

"I love you." She nodded. "No…you're my life, my heart, every part of me, you're it. I will love you for the rest of my life."

"I love you too. And want to have children with you. Fuck me, Caleb. I need you." He took her hard, harder than he had any woman before. And she continued to beg him for more. "Come."

His body responded to her command like he was on a hair trigger. As he emptied his body into hers again, she dug her nails deep into his shoulders. And when she offered her throat to him, he leaned in and bit her hard, right where her shoulder met with her neck, and tasted hot blood as it filled his mouth.

Drinking deeply of her, he felt her teeth scrape around his shoulder and waited for her bite. When it came, he felt a deeper connection to her snap into place, along with all the sensual pleasure that came from being united. It was like a rubber band at his wrist, only this was happening to his heart and mind. Sealing the wound he'd made, he waited for her to do the same as he held her to him. Honestly, he wasn't sure that he had the energy to move just then.

Somehow they made it to the bed. He wasn't sure if they walked or stumbled most of the way, and when they dropped down on the cheap mattress, both of them laughed. The bed creaked twice before it simply collapsed under their combined weight. Neither of them got up to fix it, but laid there in each other's arms.

"Hopefully that old four poster bed in our new house will hold up to our kind of sex." He kissed the top of her head when she yawned as she continued. "Also, I wasn't kidding before. I'd very much like to have a child with you. I don't know how that works, but if you'd not mind, I'd love it."

"I'd love to have as many children as you'd like. Hundreds if you have a mind to. But as for when, you'd have to go into heat, now that you're a wolf. I guess as a human, it would have been called ovulating. But when you are, you'll know before me." She asked him why. "I have no idea. Mom would know, but I'm not sure how you'd feel about asking her. She'll get all red in the face when she tells you, but she'll give you a lot of female information that I wouldn't know."

"I have no problem asking her. And I think your mom is a wonderful person. Your dad too. But you know me, I just blurt things out." He said he did, but loved that about her. "I love you too. Now, go to sleep. We have a lot going on tomorrow."

They did too. A great deal. There was the final paperwork on the house, the meeting with Daniel, as well as getting this place packed up and ready to go. Also, he needed to get some work done. He'd convinced Mr. Dorsey—he supposed he should start calling him Alexander—that in order to make his product shine, he was going to be giving away a great deal of food. Also, he needed to finish up on a brand logo. He supposed that excited him the most, to be working again.

The longer he laid there, the more thoughts of the product filled his head. He was finished with the Mercantile logo, and the bags as well as signage had been ordered. Caleb had spoken to two other potential clients over the last few days, and he was going to do some work for them. Getting up, careful not to wake Quinn, he made his way to the living room and started his computer. He had too many ideas racing around in his head to go to sleep now anyway.

125

CHAPTER 9

David was both impressed and pissed that Caleb had such a nice place. He wondered if he'd been planning this a lot longer than before he'd quit. He'd only been gone from Lancaster Advertising for a little over two weeks, and here he was with a huge facility, new desks and equipment, and a setting. The décor made it look like it was made to come in and work, but have fun too.

He'd had to make an appointment to talk to his former employee, soon to be employee again, and that had pissed him off royally. Well, everything did of late. The sign on the front of the building said opening soon, but a few questions at the local restaurant had netted him enough information to know that it was opening Monday, today. He'd had to wait for two extra days in this town just to get in to see him to talk. And now that he was here, he had a feeling that Caleb was going to need a lot more than the twenty-five cent raise he was going to dangle in front of him to get him to return

David thought about how to get Caleb to come back a great deal, because after dealing with his dad over this mess, David realized that he was right, Caleb was their business. His dad hadn't been so much pissed as he thought it was funny.

David had lost his only money maker, and his dad had

said it was about what he deserved for the way he treated him. Also, clients and employees were leaving his firm quickly now, and today, he knew why. Clients were coming here. And his other employees would soon follow where the money was. David couldn't afford that.

The conversation he'd had with his dad on Friday had pissed him off. The nerve of his dad telling him that he treated people poorly and that he was going to regret it. He'd asked his dad about the ill treatment of Caleb.

"How do you figure that? Because I made him do his job?" David had snorted at his dad. "Caleb should have been a better employee, willing to give up a few hours of his personal time to work on projects. It's not like he had a life outside of here. I don't coddle anyone, Father, you know that."

"Yes, sadly I do. But what would it have hurt you to have said a kind word to any of them? Wished them a happy birthday? I know you get the memos on those dates. I send them to you myself." David had asked what good that would do. "You mean because you're paying them? Because it matters to them. How would you like it if I simply forgot your birthday, or any holiday?"

"You're my father. You're required to give me those things. Even if, as you obviously think, I don't deserve them. What does this have to do with Caleb walking out anyway?" His dad had laughed a little, then stood up. "I suppose now you're going to blame this all on me. Well, I didn't do a damned thing but pay him to do a job he refused to do. Why, when I think on it now, I should have fired him, not let him quit."

"If you say so. And as far as being required to give you anything, that's not how it works. But I must say, I thought for sure you'd be able to hang onto this place a little longer. But since you let Caleb go—"

"He walked out. I didn't fire him. When are you going to get that into your head? I did not let him go." Again, his dad had nodded and gone to the door. "I'll get him back, Dad. See if I don't. And when I do, you'll see how I get this place back up from the ruin you think I got it in."

"Mr. Lancaster?" He looked up at the woman who called his name. He'd forgotten for a moment where he was... thinking about his dad did that to him. "Mr. Lancaster, if you're ready, Mr. Winchester can see you now. But as I said earlier, he doesn't have but a few minutes."

"This is all it will take, honey." She took a step back from him when he put out his hand. "I don't bite. Unless you want me to."

"Never. My husband would also object, so I'd back off if I were you." He laughed. Women were so coy when they thought they needed to be to get something. "Mr. Winchester is this way."

He followed her, admiring the way her hips swayed and her legs looked in the high heels she had on. As they rounded a corner, he nearly missed seeing the rest of the set up that Caleb had. But when he did, he could only stare at it all.

"Christ. This is beautiful." The woman smiled and said that they'd only just gotten it set up. "It looks like he's ready for a lot of work coming his way. How the hell did he afford this working for me?"

"I'm sure that his employment with you had nothing to do with it. But he is off to a good start. He has three clients already. While one of them isn't that big of a customer just yet, we all see the potential. Mr. Dorsey has brought a few of his—"

"Mr. Dorsey is my client." The smile disappeared and the

scowl was back. "Where is Winchester? I want to talk to him right this moment."

"Well, I'm taking you to see him. But if I were you, I'd drop the attitude. That's going to get you tossed out on your rear. Not that you might not be anyway." He growled and she did it right back to him, scaring him a great deal. "You try that again with me, buster, and they'll never find your body."

He kept his mouth shut for the rest of the walk. The nerve of some people. And now to find out that Caleb had stolen his clients. David had had a passing thought that they'd eventually come here if he didn't get the man back, but to know it for sure was aggravating. He was sure that two more of his clients would come here instead of renewing their contracts as he'd hoped they would now that he'd seen the set up here. This little venture of Caleb's was hurting him. David was going to have to have a very serious talk with the man about loyalty.

As soon as he entered the big office, he turned to the woman. This wasn't right. But before he could tell her to take him to the right room, she slammed the door in his face. David turned back to the large conference table that was filled with not just Dorsey and Winchester and a few of his clients, but David's dad as well.

"What's the meaning of this? I thought I was going to have a talk with Caleb. Dad? What's going on?" His dad only patted the seat next to him. "I don't want to sit; I want to talk to Caleb here about coming back to work. And what he's done to the business by walking out that day."

"I'm not going to work for you again, David. I thought I made that pretty clear when I left there. I've done what I should have been doing all along and working in my own business." David sat then, his knees suddenly very shaky. "I don't think you could have convinced me to come back even had I not had the means to do this."

"You can't do this to me, Caleb. Think of all the times I've covered for you." David looked at Dorsey. "He was never the great artist you thought he was. I had to have all his work redone before I sent it to you."

"Really?" David was desperate, he had to fight to get at least something from this mess. And Dorsey had been a great client of theirs. "Then I wonder who Caleb here had go over his latest work. The thing about that is, my firm? They think this is going to make it the best-selling product on the market. So, whatever you did to his work? I'm thinking you held him back. I love what he's doing for me."

David looked at his dad. "This is all your doing. You came here and set me up. How could you do that to your own son?" His dad laughed and that pissed him off more. "You bastard. You did this. You made Caleb leave the firm just so you could see me fail. Well, it won't happen. I'm going to make that company rock and me along with it."

"You don't work there anymore." David looked at Caleb when he spoke. "Lancaster Advertising is shut down as of an hour ago. I bought it, all of it, from your dad, and I've decided that I don't need the extra space right now so I'm going to hold the building, then perhaps open a branch later. But you're out of work."

"You can't do that to me. I own that place." He looked at his father again and he smiled. "Tell him that you gave me that place when you retired."

"I did. And there were stipulations in place when you took it over. You had to show a profit, which you did not. In fact, you're about two weeks from being so far in the red that it was going to go down anyway. You had to stop doing drugs was another condition that was in our contract. By the way, you have a little dust on your lip." David wiped at his mouth and saw that his dad had been right, the fucker. "And you had to keep all the clientele that were there when I turned it over to you, as well as bringing one profitable one in each year. When I was there, I had seventeen. You are down to one. And I'm pretty sure they were planning to leave as well. David, you had a successful money making business that you ignored. You snorted up your nose any profits there might have been. And you treated your employees—all of them, not just Caleb here—like shit."

"This isn't fair. I was making it work until Caleb got a burr up his ass and wanted to leave work early." Caleb said it had been well after nine that night. "So? You usually worked well after that anyway when I told you I had a project to be done. What made this one...? Oh yeah, you had a death in the family. Well, working for me trumps a death in the family, and you should have fucking known that. Your leaving the firm hurt my business, and I'm not happy about that. As for you closing me down, that's not going to happen either. Stop this right now and we'll talk like businessmen should."

"I'm done talking with you." Caleb stood up and so did David. He wasn't leaving, David wasn't finished yet. "I have to go and pick up my brother-in-law, and then I'm going to go home with my wife and unpack."

"I didn't say you could go. Sit down right now before I have you fired." David was grasping at straws, he knew it. But damn it, he wasn't going to take this. "I want you to tell me that you're not going to do this. Right now, Caleb. This is stupid."

But he didn't sit. He just kept making his way to the door as if David had not said a word. David looked back at the people at the table. Some of them he recognized, others he had no idea. He sat down again, trying to regroup, when two of the men at the table stood as well.

"What's happening here? I don't understand." His dad and he were the only two left now. He looked at him. "Why did you do this to me? I'm your son. You should have stood up for me, not torn me down like you always do."

"I didn't tear you down, David. You did that all by yourself. As for Caleb leaving you, I think it was the smartest thing he could have done. He's a good man and a great advertising agent. He can think on his feet, and he's not afraid to take chances to make something work well for his clients. You should have been telling him how much you enjoyed him coming to work for you, showing him in some way that you appreciated him and his work, instead of burying him in the office with no sunlight." He told his dad that Caleb had a view. "Yes, he does, and as usual, you're missing the point all together. What I mean is, you should have treated him with more respect. You didn't do that for any of them."

"Respect? You mean like that showed to me? Never, not once, did they ever greet me the way they used to you. I never got anyone to ask me how my weekend was, or if I had seen whatever sport was on television." His dad asked him if he'd asked them anything like that. "Why would I? I'm the boss, not their friend."

"That's where you made your first mistake, David. They were my friends. All of them. I knew their birthdates, their children's names as well as birthdays. I sent flowers when there was a death in the family, and I supported them when they needed it. The Christmas parties that we had were epic, and they respected me as much as I did them. They were more than friends; they were like my family." David told him he was his only family. "Yes, you're my son. But those people treated me better on their worse days than you have your entire life."

His dad stood up to leave and David was at a loss. What the hell was he supposed to do now? Where was he going to get the kind of cash that the firm paid him every week? He was pretty sure that Caleb wasn't going to fork over his paycheck from now on. He asked his dad.

"Pay you? No, why on earth would you think that? You don't have a job, son. Why would you think that you'd still get a check?" He told him again, for what seemed like the hundredth time, that he was his son. "You are. And as of right now, you're going to make it on your own. Also, you might want to find yourself a car and an apartment. Without a job and the firm picking up the tab, I'm pretty sure you can't afford either any longer. You really fucked up, son. And to be honest with you, I'm thrilled to death I got to see it happen. You deserve this."

He sat there after his dad left. David had no idea what he was supposed to do now. Everyone, it seemed, was out to get him. That much was obvious. But why? He felt like he was being punished, singled out for being a boss. Well, he wasn't going to take this lying down. He was going to go home right now and become the best ad-man in the business. He wasn't sure how he was going to accomplish this, but he was going to do it, by God.

~~~

"Do you think he had a good time?" Caleb said that he'd bet he had a wonderful time, for the fifth time. "I know that I've asked you that before, but he's never been away from us for this long. And I'm nervous."

"I am too." She looked at him and smiled. "He's a great

kid. And I'm so excited about him coming to live with us. Your dad too. We'll have fun. And we'll be a huge family, all of us."

"We will have fun, and with all that room, Harley won't bother you too much." She didn't think he'd be able to work around Harley, no matter how many times he told her he'd be fine. She thought it was going to be a huge change for him to be around Harley all the time. But Caleb wasn't worried. If he had to, he could go to his office for a little while to work. "You never told me what happened with Lancaster. Is he going to go away nicely?"

"Doubtful, but I don't care so long as he leaves us alone. I took on four more clients today. And I hired some staff. Not a lot, but a few." She nodded; he could tell she was still distracted. "There's the bus now."

The bus, a newer one that had padded cloth seats rather than the bus that they'd had before, pulled in. Her dad had done that for them, and Caleb was jealous that he'd not thought of it first. Dominic told him that the other bus was nearly twenty years old, and had been a donation from someone.

There was a great deal of excitement, both in the crowd waiting to pick people up and the bus load of campers. As soon as Harley saw them, he started jumping up and down and waving his hands. Caleb smiled at his enthusiasm. He hugged his sister tightly several times, then his dad. Instead of a hug for him, however, Harley took his hand. Caleb thought it was the most emotional thing that he'd ever had happen to him.

Debra and James came to talk to them almost as soon as they left the bus themselves. "He's been so excited today. I think he understood that he was going to see you guys." Quinn asked how it had gone. "He was wonderful. And we had so much fun working with him. He's very smart."

"He can fish in small increments. And he can bait his own hook now." James pulled out his phone and showed them pictures of Harley at the camp as he continued. "He was only in trouble once. And after an hour of washing dishes, he decided that he liked the job enough to stick around and help every day. And before you ask, the trouble he got into wasn't that bad. He didn't want to take a shower on the first day. After that, it was great."

"He usually is so good about that. After we help him wash his hair, he's been doing his own washing." Quinn told them she was sorry.

"Don't be sorry. It shows his independence. He didn't want to take a shower, and I think it was only that he was nervous about being around strangers. We dealt with it and he did much better afterwards." He took back his phone and smiled. "I would like to talk to you about having him go to the school that we have set up here in town. It would be good for him to be in a social setting that's structured. I mean, he did very well in crafts and games. He can fish, which I don't think he's done before. He's very smart, as we said, and I think we can help him with his skills."

"We've been working with him." James said that it showed, that Harley, for his mental disabilities, his skills were far beyond what most people with was autism were. "Thank you. We have help, and Dad and I, we make sure that we get him out in public as much as we can. So he doesn't get tired of just seeing us."

"He liked it there, then?" Debra told Alexander that she thought he had a very good time. "Then I see no reason for him not to have some day time with you people too. I mean, he sure looks happy. I want the best for him."

Caleb was very proud of them both. It would be hard for them to let someone else take some of the responsibility for Harley over for them. But he thought Harley looked great. He had a tan on his face, he was smiling a great deal, and he was calmer.

When they were on their way home, he suggested they hit the restaurant. He'd made arrangements with the owner to make sure that Harley would get some crispy fries when he came in from now on, and he was hungry. As soon as they sat down, Milly came over and took their order. When she was gone, Alexander asked if he could come by his offices later. He had a deal for him.

"Of course. Anytime. By the way, your print work is finished and I sent it to your company man as you asked. All we have to do now is set up a few ads in the paper, as well as some online and televisions ads." Caleb could tell that he was distracted, so he moved on to more mundane things, and not about the business. "The house is going to be finished up by the time we get there this afternoon. All the rooms have been given a nice clean up, not that it really needed it, but—"

"How do you suppose those people pay for all those kids going out there all the time?" Caleb took the change of subject with ease. "I mean, it has to be very expensive having those helpers there. A doctor on staff. Do they have grants? Money from the government?"

"They're running it on donations for the most part. The staff is all volunteers that have had or has a student there at some point in their lives. The new bus was much needed, and a great relief to them. They won't have to cancel outings if the bus were to break down, thanks to you. Which, I've been told, happened more often than not. Also, the pack that is nearby keeps the lawns trimmed as well as poachers out that might try and hurt the people there. And so you know, there hasn't been much trouble at this place, but it does happen on occasion." Alexander nodded and asked him about day to day expenses. "My family has donated foodstuff. The local churches as well as the clubs that are in town donate time and food as well. Power is paid for by the pack, I believe, but Daniel said it is a small price to pay considering how much they do for the people who need it."

"And the school? James said that there is one in town. How do they fund that one?" Caleb said he didn't know about that, but he knew that Dominic worked there in the summer months. "I'll talk to him then. I want to donate. Maybe set up some sort of trust for them to use. You know anything about that sort of thing?"

"No, but my mom might. She worked for an attorney for years before we were all born. Retired for some years, but I bet she'd know how to get you in touch with someone that could help you." Alexander said he'd give her a call. "I can do you one better. How about you come over to dinner tonight? The family gets together once a week no matter what we're up to so we can keep in touch. I think they'd love to have you there."

"I don't want to intrude." Caleb told him he'd be welcome with open arms. "Well, I'd like that. I guess I can talk to her then. I'm also thinking of other ways we can help this foundation out. Fundraisers and such."

"They could use all the help they can get, I think." He nodded and smiled when Harley's fries were set in front of him. "He likes them this way, and there isn't any reason to upset him when it's as simple as putting them in the fryer a little longer."

They enjoyed their meal and a few people came by to talk

to him about the Mercantile. Caleb had invested in it for Sally Anne. The building they were using was perfect, but they needed better equipment as well as capitol to start up. He'd been so happy with the results. When the banker told them they could expect in the first year, he was glad to be in on the ground floor.

"Heard any more about that wolf?" Caleb said that he had and that they had a plan working. "I was talking to the alpha here. He seems to think that there is more going on with this feller than the rest might know about. He said he had someone watching him at all times."

"Yes. He told me. The pack is making sure that when he is in his other form that they keep others away. Especially in garages and open fields. I think we've been hurting his play time a little." Alexander asked about the alpha position. "Quinn and I have talked about it, but I'm still not sure I'm the man for the job."

"I think you'd be perfect for it. I'm assuming you've not told your parents yet." Caleb said his dad would assume he was taking it, so he wanted to have his ducks lined up first. "Yes, I have noticed that your dad can get a little ahead of himself at times. But he's a good man and about the smartest man I've met in a while. He knows his stuff when it comes to being a people person."

"He does. My dad spends a lot of time around a lot of different kinds of people. Humans and supernaturals. And he's not the type that would talk your arm off either. He says what he wants then moves on. To see him sit and talk with you for hours on end, it's strange. But he really seems to enjoy it." Alexander said he did as well. "You should talk to him about fishing. He rarely did it when we were younger, but he talked about it a great deal. I bet he'd jump at the chance to take you and Harley out sometime."

Quinn squeezed his thigh under the table. They had a date tonight. She was going to go into the woods and shift for the first time. Daniel had finally okayed her to be strong enough to do it, and she was excited and nervous about it. So was he. He had a feeling, however, that she was going to be a beautiful she-wolf.

CHAPTER 10

Wade moved between the cars of the garage and tried to get a fix on the woman that had just left the elevator. He'd not been having a lot of luck at things of late. Just yesterday he'd been let go from his job. They were doing budget cuts, and since he was considered unnecessary staff, he'd been let go. The bastards.

But he thought it left him more time for his other activities. And until the last few days, it had been fun. But now it was as if someone was warning people to be more careful. He hadn't touched a woman in three days now, and he was pissed off. Someone was going to pay for his misery, and pay big time.

Wade heard the click-click of heels and hunkered down to leap. But when he saw the woman, he knew it wasn't the one that he was after. This one was older, her body simply worn out by age and just being a human. As he made his way around the car he'd been by, he paused when a scent touched his nose. Lifting his snout up, he tried to take more of it in until he recognized it. It was a woman…one of his women.

It wasn't fresh, but it had been recent. As he sniffed his way to the spot that he was smelling, he tried to think which one woman it had been. It wasn't easy, not really. He'd bitten a great many women in his time. Just as he was getting close to the smell, the elderly woman stepped in front of him.

Wade wasn't sure who was more surprised, her or him, but when she opened her mouth to scream, Wade did the only thing he could...he leapt at her. He could have run, he supposed, but it was much too late for that when she went down. And since she was under him and had caused him so much trouble, he had some fun—well, his sort of fun—with her.

The taste of hot fear-filled blood enraged his wolf. As he tore more into her warm flesh, Wade felt wonderful. Younger than he had in years. He let the savage part of him do whatever he wanted. Blood sprayed over him, filled his mouth and caught on his fur. The smell of it, fresh and hot, made him want more, to cause more damage to her, and he did, just doing what he thought came natural to his kind.

When he'd done all the mutilation that he could, leaving her frail body open to the elements, he did something that he'd not done in decades. He stood over his prey and howled. He felt exhilarated, empowered, and like the savage that he always wanted to be.

Finished with her, he'd begun moving between the cars again when he heard someone coming toward him and his prey. Wade knew that he was going to catch some shit for this. There wasn't any way another wolf would not know it was him. He would have left his scent everywhere on the woman and in the garage. Wade thought he might be better off leaving the area for a bit, until things cooled down at least.

Once he was back at his shabby apartment, he stripped down and stepped into the shower. It was quick, the hot water only lasting long enough for him to take a two minute wash up, but it was exciting to see the blood swirling around the drain from his kill. It was only in his hair, of course, since he'd shifted, but he mourned the loss of it. He thought he might take the time do this it again, and soon. It had been too much fun not to.

After dressing, he made his way to the kitchen. He wasn't terribly hungry after feeding on the woman, but he did pour himself a glass of water. Sitting at the table, he thought of what had just happened for him.

He'd killed before, of course. Over his lifetime there had been many deaths that he'd been directly and sometimes indirectly responsible for. Several times only to take over a pack, at which times he would then kill off all the families left behind. But for the most part, he'd killed for a reason. Someone had come upon him and raised a gun. Or once, long ago, he'd killed a man who had trapped on his land, all in the name of being a wolf. But not today. Today had been for himself.

He'd killed because he could. There wasn't any reason for him to have torn the woman apart. She hadn't been any sort of personal threat to him. She would have screamed, but he was faster than her and any police that would have eventually shown up. But he had killed and he had enjoyed it. Immensely.

As he sat there, thinking again about the way he'd felt, he heard someone on the streets below. Getting up, he looked out the window and saw four men there, all of them looking up to where he was standing. Wondering what it was about, he leaned down to open the window when it shattered over his head, raining glass over his body, Wade jumped back.

Ceiling tile fell on his head as he lay there, cowering like a child. The sound reverberated again and again as what he knew now were shots being fired. They tore at the walls and his furniture as if it was nothing. He crawled on his belly to the living room, really just an expansion of the kitchen, to hide

143

behind the couch.

It went on for ten minutes. Sirens could be heard in the distance, but it didn't seem to stop the onslaught of shots being fired into his little rooms. Even as the sound of police coming grew closer, the noises never stopped. He figured there must have been as many as fifty or more bullets ripping through his things.

The last sound, the sound of something heavy hitting the floor, made him think of bombs and grenades. He had no idea why those thoughts popped into his head, but they were there now and he couldn't unthink them. Then the pounding at his door began.

"Police. Open up." He wasn't stupid enough to think they were going to help him. "Mr. Douglas, are you in there?"

He didn't answer, but did crawl on his belly to his bedroom. Wade had to get out of there, now. As soon as he made it to his closet, his door exploded open and heavy boots pounded on the floor. He was just opening the smallish door that would get him into the next apartment when he heard more guns being fired. These were so close that he was sure they were firing at him. The door was closing to his escape hole when they entered his bedroom. Wade watched them move around his room through the crack in the boards.

One thing was very clear, however. These men were not police, and they weren't human. He'd just been found by the Wolf Council, and was sure they weren't there about his past due dues. He also realized that he had to get moving. As wolves themselves, they'd find where he'd gone and kill him now that they had his scent.

Wade gathered his stash as he entered the next rooms. No one had lived in the neighboring apartment for nearly six years, and he'd made use of it. He was sure that the entire place was just one brick crumbling from becoming a heap on the sidewalk, but it had served him well over the years and he hoped it would today as well. He picked up his bag and a change of clothing. Dressing in the fourth apartment from his, he tried to think how they'd found him so quickly. Then it hit him. That guy.

The man from the other day that had threatened him. He had to be it. There wasn't any other person with enough balls to have turned him in. Wade was an alpha after all, and things like that carried a penalty. He was going to find the bastard and kill him. Wade was going to avenge himself.

It took him nearly an hour to get to the parking garage where he'd seen the man. Another fifteen minutes to find his car. His scent was his now, and Wade was going to make his own kind of justice. Waiting in the shadows, he thought that he might come to like this sort of fun. Killing like the animal he was certainly gave him a much better thrill than just biting a bunch of stupid bitches.

The man came out of the elevator with several other people. He thought about killing them all, just for the fun of it, but realized that while he was feeling good about himself, he was still a slightly older man, and might not survive against six grown, younger men. Wade might still be high on his latest kill, but he wasn't stupid. But his caution was for nothing, as the men as one turned and looked at him.

"Hello, Wade. How's it hanging?" He didn't move out of the darkness he was in, but he had a feeling that they could still see him. "I thought I told you not to come around here again. You're not going to be hurting anyone else while I'm around."

"Really? Perhaps you don't know all of my haunts." He came out of the shadows just enough that they could see him.

145

"And I'll go where I want, when I want. You are nothing but a pup compared to my knowledge and strength."

They looked at each other, and he knew they were afraid now. An alpha like him was not one to take lightly. But when they started laughing, at him, he felt his rage take him. And just like before, his wolf wanted blood. Letting his body go, he watched in horror as they too shifted.

A bear, cougar, and a tiger were with the wolf. There was a lion and panther as well, and they leapt at him at once. Wade knew he was going to die, but he was going to take as many of them as possible with him when he did.

~~~

Frank Durham waited outside the building for twenty or so minutes. He was bleeding badly, but nothing a shift and a good run wouldn't help. He'd be weak…it was the reason that he'd come here instead of going home first. He needed to let the man in charge of his pack know what he'd done. Well, what they'd done. But the others, they had their own pack masters to talk to.

"Yes?" He looked up at his alpha and dropped to his belly. "What have you done, Frank? Christ, is that all your blood?"

No. It's a few of us. We found the guy that's been hurting the woman. He was told to come in and then shift. As he was being handed a pair of pants to pull on, Frank explained. "The guy that's been biting those women, I found him a few days ago. Warned him off, but apparently, he didn't think I was serious."

"What did you do the first time you saw him, and why didn't you tell me?" Frank could hear the anger in his voice and he dropped to his knees. He heard Daniel exhale loudly, but he didn't move. "I'm sorry. This man, what did you do to him? Today, I mean."

146

"He was hiding in the shadows when me and a few of my friends were leaving tonight. I don't know who smelled him first, but we all turned to look where he was hiding. But it wasn't just his scent. He had.... Well, death was all over him. It wasn't until I was almost here that I remembered seeing a story about a woman that had been mauled to death today in the mall parking garage." Daniel asked if he confessed. "No. Not to us, not verbally. But he was the one, we all knew it."

"Unfortunately, your knowing it, no matter how true, will not stand up in court. Christ, this is a cluster fuck." Frank had to agree, but he was surprised by his alpha saying it aloud. "You've met Caleb Winchester, haven't you? Kelley's oldest boy?"

"Yes. His brother Owen and I went to high school together. If you don't mind me asking, what does he have to do with this?" Frank listened as he was told about the mate to Caleb being bitten and nearly dying. "Christ. He's out there marking women for no other reason than he can."

"That pretty much sums it up. And now, if what you're saying is true, he's decided to kill along with it." Daniel started pacing and Frank sat very still. He wasn't dumb enough to think that he'd ask for help or advice, and he didn't want to overstep his bounds. This man was a good leader, but he was also deadly. "I need to talk to Caleb. I'd like for you to come with me. You can do that, right?"

"Yes. Whatever you need, I can do for you." Frank watched him pace faster, his mind working, no doubt, as quickly as his hands were. He'd never noticed that before, how Daniel talked a great deal with his hands in motion. "I might know where he lives."

Frank had no idea why he said that. It just spilled out while his mind was working out the hand movements. But

Daniel didn't seem to care that he'd only thought it and not meant to say it. He asked him where it was.

"There are a bunch of buildings in the downtown area. Most of them are run down enough that they have eviction notices on them." Daniel asked if he knew which one Wade was in. "Yes. Well, sort of. We followed him to one that is still a rental, but we lost him in the crowd. The police had a guard or two hanging around the building when we got there."

"Police? Were they looking for him too?" Frank rubbed his head. It was his habit when he was nervous, much like his alpha flaying his hands about. "What is it? What were they doing there?"

"I'm not so sure they were the police. They looked like them, had on uniforms that all looked official, but they didn't look right." Daniel asked him what he meant, just as patient as he was when he talked to his little girl. "There was this logo on them. Not like the police wear. Here, let me draw it for you."

Frank started searching through the pants he had on, completely forgetting they weren't his. Daniel handed him a notepad and pen, and he closed his eyes to try and remember every detail about the logo. When he was sure he had it, Frank drew it as best he could for his alpha.

"Good Christ." When Daniel fell back on his chair, Frank thought for sure he'd done something wrong. Perhaps he'd remembered it a little off. But when he asked him about it, Daniel just shook his head. "Give me a minute while this sinks in."

Frank was worried and did stupid things when he was. Moving to the little fridge that he saw in the corner, he got himself and Daniel a bottle of water. He was nearly finished drinking his, draining it, when he realized how presumptuous he'd been. He apologized.

"Don't. Please don't. You did nothing that wasn't helpful. But this drawing.... Do you have any idea who this is?" He said that he didn't. "It's the PC, or Paranormal Council. Not just the Wolf Council, but these guys are working for the council that governors all paranormals. If they're here and looking for Wade, then things are a bit more complicated than we thought. And a great deal more deadly for our buddy Wade. Christ, he must have really fucked up if they're here. I mean, more than biting women and killing a few humans."

"You think they're here to take him in." Daniel told him he thought they would kill him rather than do that. "And these guys I saw, they're the hit man for the PC? They were armed to the teeth, I can tell you that."

"They would be, I would imagine. And I'd bet that they had nothing but silver and iron on them, to take out anything that they might encounter." Frank started pacing then and rubbing his head. "We have to talk to Caleb. He has to know what's going on too."

"I don't want to tell him this. The other, that I knew where he might be, was bad enough, but...sheesh, he'll eat me alive. Literally." Frank realized that his voice had taken a sharp turn; he sounded like a teenager going through puberty. He'd also told his boss no. "What I mean is, I'd rather not tell him. I like Owen a great deal and we go running a lot, but his brother scares the crap out of me. I hate to bring this up right now, but if he would challenge you for your territory, I'd just hand it over to him. He's scary strong."

"I offered it to him. Twice this week, as a matter of fact. He's turned me down." Frank asked why. "You mean why did I offer it? Or he didn't take it? Both reasons for us is the same. Our family. We both want.... No, we both need to spend

149

more time with our families. And as much as I'd like to say I can talk him into this, I don't think I'm having much luck. I thought about enlisting his dad's help, but I've not done it yet."

"Mr. Winchester would about bust his buttons if Caleb were to take the position." Frank felt bad again for acting like he didn't want Daniel to be his alpha. "You've done a good job. We have jobs that we didn't before. And money in the pot if we need it. There is even that committee that you set up to help with the elderly that is working well. My mom loves to have those younger pups, she calls them, come in and give her home a nice once over. But Caleb...Caleb is a great man, a good brother to his family, but he's not you. What I mean is, while you do things for the pack that benefits, Caleb would be a monster protecting us."

"I can't do that." Frank shook his head sadly. "I never knew if it was my being a doctor that prevented me from being a monster, as you call it, or the fact that it's just not in me. I'd like to think that if push came to shove I could, but I really don't see it happening."

"Nah, me either." Daniel laughed and Frank felt his face heat up. "I'm sorry. My mouth and my head, they don't converse much when I'm talking. It's like the words are in my head and while I'm thinking I should rephrase them or something, they just spill on out like my granny's coffee in her broken pot."

"You should buy her another pot. I was over there a few days ago, and she had to make three pots of that brew of hers before we each got a cup. To see her hurrying over with that hot stuff is scarier than Caleb is." They both laughed. "I did offer to get her one and she told me that one was just fine. What a woman."

"She is at that. Granny sure does like to pinch pennies. And she'd squeeze a dollar until it hollered." Frank sat down, feeling better for changing the subject. "What are you going to tell Caleb? I'm sure he's not going to be thrilled to know that they're around."

"Maybe. But knowing they're here is going to be better than running into them when they're working. I would imagine that whoever sent them, they're going to do their job well." Frank certainly hoped so. "We'll have to report that you've run into Wade, if for no other reason than they'll smell you on him. The others too. I'd hate for them to think that you are with the man. And while I don't know these men or the others that do this job, I have a feeling that they'd not ask questions until you were dead."

"No, we don't want that. I sure do like living, just so you know." Frank sat there for a few more minutes. "This PC, what do you think they've figured out? I mean, there must be something that brought them here, right? And they were at the complex today before much could have been found out about that lady's death."

"I don't know, but I'm sure that we'll find out soon enough. I just...the thought of calling someone and letting them know what's going on is a little more than I wanted to do today."

Frank stayed until Daniel made two phone calls. The first was to Caleb, and he was on his way over. The second was to the Wolf Council. They would have to be informed that the Paranormal Council might be in town. Daniel said he'd have to call their bosses first and hoped that they'd volunteer to make the call. But of course, like him, they were afraid. So, Daniel was to make the call.

Caleb arrived with his lovely wife about ten minutes into

151

the conversation with the PC. Frank filled them in on what was going on, what he had found out, and who Daniel was talking with. Quinn sat down and looked a little pale, so Frank lowered his voice a little more to speak to Caleb. He knew she could hear them, but he didn't want to upset her much more.

"Wade killed a woman at the mall earlier. Her body showed up around noon today." Frank said that was more than likely the blood he'd smelled on Wade. "That would be my guess as well. When you guys attacked him, did you hurt him badly enough that he might need medical help? I can only hope that he crawled in a hole somewhere and died."

"I doubt he'd be all that accommodating." They both turned to Daniel when he spoke. "I just got off the phone with the PC. They're telling us to stand down, they have this. Also, we're to keep it to ourselves that they're in town. I hope you don't mind, Frank, but I told him that I saw them, not you."

"Fine by me. I'd like to lay as low as I can with this one." Quinn laughed when the rest of them did, but she looked afraid. Frank went to talk to her. "I'm sorry about this, missus. But you know that we'll do everything in our power to keep you safe from this guy. Of course, I'd hate to be him when he thinks to come after you. I'm sure you can tear him apart."

"I hope so. I've not had an opportunity to shift just yet." He told her he'd just heard that she'd been hurt. And Frank wondered if the pack knew she'd been nearly killed by an infection from Wade. He doubted it; for some reason he thought that had they known, Wade would have died weeks ago. "I think, now more than ever, I need to get on this. First thing."

"Yes, ma'am, I'd sure try and get some control over my wolf if I was you. She'll be fine too. So will you." He also told her she'd be a pretty wolf too.

152

Frank wasn't a learned man. Nor was he stupid. But if and when Wade came calling — and he knew that the dumbass would — he'd be having his ass handed back to him in a shake of a lambs tail, as his granny used to say. He'd not fuck with the Winchesters on a good day. Wade was taking it to a whole new level of shit storms.

CHAPTER 11

Caleb wanted to tell her again that it was fine if she was afraid and that she would be all right. But she'd threatened him twice already, and he was reasonably sure that she'd not just say how pissed she was at him for repeating himself, and act against his body. But the longer she stood there, just staring at the trees, the more he wanted to shift himself to show her.

"When he came at me — Wade, I mean — when he came at me, all I could think about was he was going to tear my throat out. That I was as good as dead." He waited, sure she was just speaking and not requiring him to answer just yet. "Then when he knocked me down, tore at my body, it was as if every horror movie and story I'd ever read or seen was coming to life. He was fucking huge and his teeth were dark…bloodied, I think now. And I remember thinking that my dad wouldn't be able to identify my body, they'd have to use dental records to do it."

"He's huge because of what he is. Or was. You have no idea how glad I am that he didn't kill you. You're all I want in this world, Quinn." She turned and looked at him and he saw the tears on her cheeks. "I'd like nothing more than to tell you we can do this some other time. That we have all the time in the world. But we don't. Not with him killing women now.

You must be able to shift comfortably and quickly in the event that he comes for you. And he will."

"Because he knows somehow that you found me and took me. Like it was any of his business in the first place." He nodded. "Why does he even care? It's not like he could claim me for his own, could he? I mean, I belong to you in a way. Why would he even try?"

"There is no reason for him to care or to try and make a claim on you in the first place. He did it simply because in some sick way, it gave him some pleasure, I'm guessing. Honey, there wasn't any reason for him to bite any of the people he did. Just like there was no reason for him to kill. He does it because he can. And the fact that he's gotten away with it for so long has made him braver...or stupider; it would depend on how you looked at it." He held her then, let her cry on his chest while it felt as if his heart was being ripped apart because of it. "Close your eyes. Can you see her? She is waiting on you to release her."

"I'm afraid." He said he was there with her. Nothing would harm her so long as he held her. "You're awfully sure of yourself there, big boy."

Caleb laughed and felt some of his tension go away with it. Kissing her on the mouth quickly, he stepped back from her and let his own wolf take him. He stood before her and waited for her to join him.

If you shift, I can take you out beyond those trees and show you how wolves mate. She cocked a brow at him. *They're very vocal and hard on each other, but I'll make it up to you as soon as you take back your human form and we both have you. From what I've heard, it's not all that enjoyable for the female.*

"From what you've heard, huh? I suppose the next thing you tell me is that you've never had sex before me." He laughed, but didn't answer her. "Just what I thought. Okay, here I go."

The shift was beautiful. Caleb had seen his brothers shift, several thousand times he'd bet, but to see Quinn do it was magical. Her body wasn't just consumed by her wolf, but seemed to separate and become the wolf. Caleb stared at her when he realized something else about her wolf.

I'm ugly, aren't I? He could only shake his head. *Either tell me or I'm going to just become me again and be done with you.*

You're white. Like fresh snow is. I've never seen a white wolf before. She shook her head, her big wolf as disbelieving as he was. *I knew you'd be special, that your wolf would be as well, but I never dreamed in a million years that you'd be this special. Oh, Quinn, you're the most beautiful wolf I have ever seen.*

You're just saying that.

They both turned when someone slammed a door on the porch. It was her dad and Harley. Harley was staring at them both as if he had been given a gift. His running to them made Caleb realize how much he already loved the kid. His excitement was infectious too.

Yes, he was an adult, but he would never have the actions of one. He was still wearing a diaper, had to be dressed and undressed and even bathed. Sometimes his eating habits were messy. But he was happy most of the time, and he loved with all his heart. As he approached Quinn, his steps a little slower, Caleb sat down and watched them.

They were both soon jumping and running around the yard. Harley's laughter was mingled with the soft woof of Quinn's wolf. Quinn would knock him down then leap away when he got up. Harley would curl his fingers into her soft fur and wave his hands. It was as if he knew it was his sister and she'd never harm him. Then he approached his wolf.

Caleb didn't move. He just lay very still while he sat beside him. His hand moved over his forehead then down his nose. It was soft, almost as if he didn't want to harm or startle him. When Harley laid his forehead to his, Caleb looked deeply into the young man's eyes and saw not just understanding from him, but love too. Licking him on the throat, he tasted his scent and realized that Harley was offering him whatever he wanted to take.

They sat that way for ten minutes or more. Just the three of them, sitting close together while Alexander sat on the deck taking pictures with his phone. And when Harley yawned the second time, Caleb rolled to his back and let him lay on his belly. He was asleep in less than five minutes. Alexander came to stand close to them.

"He had a bad day today. The nurse said that he was in a sour mood when she tried to get him to dress, and it got worse after that." Caleb could only nod to the elderly man, so he did it to show him that he understood what he was saying. "I've never seen him so happy like this. I mean, he's normally a good kid, but out here, with the two of you, I think it might be the best medicine that you could have given him."

When Alexander went back to the deck, Caleb slipped out from under the boy and moved to the side of the house with his tear-away pants in his mouth. As he came back around the house, having shifted and dressed, he sat at the table that Alexander was at. The two of them watched Quinn and Harley as they sunned and napped in the grass.

"She was afraid of her wolf. I think seeing Harley accept her so readily gave her more confidence. So, I guess in effect, they were good for each other today." Alexander nodded. "When are you going to tell her?"

"Tell her?" Alexander blushed brightly. "I should have

known that someone would figure it out. Who told you? That doctor friend of yours?"

"No. I can smell the chemo on you. Quinn might be able to smell it too, but she's not figured it out. At least I don't think so." He nodded. "You're very sick, aren't you?"

"Yes. Three months ago, they gave me six months. I was going to tell her, but I kept thinking that they were wrong and I could beat this. Then the day before yesterday I went to see the doctor again, and he told me that it's advanced. I might have only a few weeks left." Caleb said he was sorry. "So am I. I'm glad she has you, but I wish she.... Well, very selfish of me, but I wish I'd been able to hold one of her children in my arms. Or seen her pregnant. I'm going to miss so much."

He broke down then, his sobs being masked by the hand over his mouth. Tears streamed down his weathered cheeks as he cried as quietly as he could. To see a man as strong as Alexander crying like this nearly broke him in two. Caleb touched his hand to his and Alexander grasped it like a lifeline.

"We can help you." He looked at him. "Daniel is a strong wolf. An alpha. With his permission and help, we can change you. If you'd like." Caleb had another thought, one that was less permanent. "Alexander, I have a friend, a very good friend, that I think can help you more. If you'd be willing to meet with her."

"I'd do just about anything to beat this." Caleb told him he'd contact her tonight. "If you don't mind me asking, who or what is she?"

"Vampire." Alexander paled a little, then nodded. "She's very old. Set in her ways, and sort of a pain in the ass. She's opinionated, hard headed, and one of my best friends. If she can, she'll save you for us."

"I'd like to meet with her, just to see what she can do. If

159

I can…. I was going to say hang on for a few months, I'd be happy with that, but honestly, I want it all." Caleb said he could understand that. "I'm sure you can. Yes, I'd like for you to set up a meeting or whatever you can do. Tell her that I'll pay her whatever she wants. It means that much to me."

"I doubt that she'll want much. She's been around a while and has seen it all. But I will tell you this, you must tell Quinn. Today." He looked out at Alexander's two children, both of whom would be devastated to lose this man. And so would he. "She needs to know what you're doing, as well as how bad it is. I won't go behind her back, not on something like this."

"Yes, if she found out…. If I died and she found out that you knew, she'd be royally pissed. If I live and she finds out… well, let's just say that either way, she's not going to be happy with either of us." Caleb thought that was an understatement, but only nodded. "You go ahead and talk to your friend, I'll talk to my children. I think your way is the best way."

"I believe so as well." As he sat there, watching Alexander make his way to his family like a man walking to the gallows, he felt the soft touch of another wolf. It was Daniel.

The PC is coming to your house tomorrow night. They wanted to meet with you here, but I asked that it be at your home. Not that I care if they see my house, but yours is much nicer. They both laughed, a nervous sort of laugh. *When they arrive, my wife and children will be there, as well as my second. Charlie is about to wet himself, he's so terrified they're going to come here with guns blazing.*

I doubt they work that way. And unless he's on their list, he shouldn't have anything to worry about. Daniel said that there was always something with Charlie. *Isn't that the truth?*

The two men talked about a few other things, nothing too stressful. They were both, regardless of what they were saying, a little overwhelmed by all this. Caleb told him about some things at the house.

We hired a cook today, so we'll have something other than microwaved hot wings and boiled eggs. Neither one of us like to cook, it seems. Daniel said he'd bring dessert then. *Good deal. What should we expect?*

To be honest, I'm not sure. I know that they'll have questions as well as some theories. The guy I spoke to, Tommy Luna, said that Wade has been in their books for a long time. It was on the tip of my tongue to ask them why they'd not taken care of him, but I decided that I didn't want to go there just yet. Caleb laughed. *And so you know, I sort of threw you under the bus. I told them I was ready to retire and pursue my career as a doctor, and that you'd make a good replacement.*

All right. Daniel laughed and said he'd expected fireworks. *I talked to Quinn…a great deal, as a matter of fact. She said that I should do it before someone came in and took it that we didn't like or trust. This way, she told me, everyone knows me and what I'm like, so it should be easier on the pack.*

I knew that I liked that girl. And she's right. Everyone knows you. However, a few of them are terrified of you. One conversation I've had recently told me that while I was a good leader, you were a monster and would get the job done. Caleb wasn't sure he liked that reference, but David explained. *He said that while I do things for the pack that benefits them all, you'd be a monster protecting us all. I think he is right.*

Caleb didn't know what to say. He didn't want to be thought of as a monster, not in any way, but to have someone believe that he'd protect them so harshly was wonderful. He asked if they were coming for dinner or just snack food.

I'd think dinner. They're arriving there about five to five-thirty tomorrow night. They said that they wanted to talk, relax, and find the lay of the land. I take it they're not from around here. Caleb said he thought they were from another country. *That would explain some things. He asked about high tea. Anyway, they said that they'd come by jet, and I had to give them information on the airport. I guess they wanted to get some input on where we might think Wade will be hiding out as well. I told them we had ideas, but no known knowledge about the man.*

They knew for the most part where he had been, but not where he was now. Caleb knew that Daniel had a lot of his men out looking for the little fucker too. When Daniel asked him to hang on, he felt like he should be listening to music. But when he came back, Caleb knew something had happened.

They found another woman's body. It's one on the list of being bitten by him. There was a man with her; he was torn up pretty badly, but he didn't know the victim. Charlie is looking into where the other women are now. Caleb asked what he could do. *Protect your mate. If he's figured out that she has a mate and that it's you, he's going to come for her next. God only knows what he might do to her when he finds out that the council is in town.*

Closing the connection, he went into the house knowing that for now, Quinn was as safe as she could be. He needed to talk to the cook, and he wanted to give Quinn and her dad some time. It was going to be hard on them all if he passed. Caleb had come to love the old man very much.

After figuring out a menu of sorts, he asked the cook what they were having for dinner tonight. When he flushed brightly, Caleb was almost afraid to ask what had happened.

"Your wife said she wanted pizza, and I'm to grill it. I've been looking on the food channels to see what I could find, and there is a great deal of information, but no real set way. I'm going to wing it." Caleb laughed when Howard did. "I do enjoy speaking with your wife, Mr. Caleb. She is a joy to be around."

"She is at that. I'm going to go to my office. She and her dad are in the yard talking. Will you let me know when they come in or if they send in Harley? I can mind him while they finish up." Howard told him he'd do that and Caleb headed to his new office.

Every time he came in here, he had the same reaction. Unbelievable. This was all his, and he still had trouble believing it. As he pulled up his work from earlier today, he thought about the holidays in this home. They were going to be loud and exciting.

A little while later, Harley came into his office with a laugh and scream. He seemed to enjoy hearing himself, and Caleb had to smile. Howard was hot on his heels as Harley sat in the chair across from him and laughed. The kid seemed to always be so alive with his happiness.

When Howard left them with cheese and crackers, he sat with Harley to help him manage the cheese. When he'd eaten about four of the treats, Caleb peeled the apple for him. While he did this, he spoke to him.

"Did you like the wolf? Your sister is beautiful, isn't she?" He smiled and took the slice of apple. "White wolves are very rare. I knew that Quinn was going to be beautiful, but I never considered she'd be as rare to everyone else as she is to me. A diamond."

They ate the apple, Harley taking small bites and drooling. Every time he could Caleb would clean him up, but it never bothered him. The quiet of the room, the fireplace roaring in the corner, lulled the younger man to sleep, and before he knew it, Harley was heading for the sofa in his office and rolling up in a blanket left there for him.

His dad came by just as he was setting things up again,

and Caleb led him to the living room where they could talk. His dad was a loud speaker, never thinking that his voice carried as well as it did. As soon as they sat down, his dad hopped right back up again and started talking.

"She never had a chance." He asked her who he was talking about. "That girl that Wade went and killed off today. Did you know her?"

"No. I only know her name because we had someone looking into who they might be." Dad huffed at him. "I have paperwork on her, but nothing else. Tell me what you might know."

"She was crossing the street and this big wolf just comes out of nowheres and takes her to the ground. They got him on tape, Caleb. Something for people to play back any time the itch to do it comes over them. Then he dragged her off to an alley with some guy chasing after him. Didn't make it to the hospital. The man bled to death trying to be a good soul." Dad stopped talking and went to the window, and Caleb knew that he was seeing Quinn. "Holy jingle bells, Caleb. Your mate is white, and look at them eyes of hers."

"I know. She doesn't believe me when I tell her how beautiful she is." He went to the window to look out with Dad. "I had Alexander tell her how sick he is. I don't think she's taking it well."

She looked up at them then and he could see her eyes. They were as green as the grass she was lying on. Her dad was rubbing her head while he spoke. It was a perfect picture, a connection between wolf and human, if the story behind it all wasn't so devastating.

"I hoped he'd come to you about it. I was thinking on that too. You should call up that girl you know, Carmen. Sure would give him a fighting chance should she give him a sip or two of herself." He told him that he'd already spoken to Alexander about it, and he was going to talk to Carmen later tonight. "That girl, she's been around a bit and some, hasn't she?"

"Yes. I think she's a few hundred years old." She was closer to being two thousand years old, but he didn't tell his dad that. Carmen was a very private and very strong vampire, and if people knew her age, they'd come for her simply because to say they hurt or killed her would be a great coup. "Like I said, I'm going to contact her tonight. I guess Alexander's doctors didn't give him long to live. And if we can help him, that'll be easier on Quinn. He told me that he wants to see her big with our child and to hold it once before he died."

"Can't think that there'd be anything better than holding a grandchild. Just to think on it, it makes me teary. But that disease, it's nasty stuff that cancer. I don't know how humans can stand it. I guess a lot of them don't and end it themselves. Just as sad, but I think maybe they think there wasn't any other way." He snorted again. "Seems to me that you'd be a hurting your family a bit more doing that, but then that's just me."

"Dad, what about the man and woman? You were going to tell me about it." His dad turned to him, his face all worked up again. "Daniel let me know it happened, but not any details."

"She was tore up. Like he was taking his anger out on her body. Poor thing. Never stood a chance. I'm thinking, from reports that had she had a gun, there wasn't any time for her to even pull the trigger, he was on her so fast. And that man." Dad shook his head. "Broke his neck, it looked like, then took his throat out later. Probably did it after he finished up with the woman. Can you imagine watching that wolf kill somebody

165

when there weren't a darn thing you could do about it? Dad burn wolf. He's going to give us all a bad time of this. They'll be hunting us for sure now. Might be hard to have a good run with all this going on. I'm thinking it'll be some time afore it's done too. What do you think on it?"

"Since they have video, then yes, it will be a long while before it's over. Someone somewhere will run it on a social media page and it'll be shared so many times, in every country, that wolves everywhere will be a target." He was afraid for Quinn and her white fur. Dad asked him if Daniel was taking precautions.

Caleb hadn't thought of that and contacted Daniel to let him know to tell the pack to be extra careful, even on their own land. Someone, a fool, would step into pack land and find himself dead if he tried to take one of them out. And more than likely a wolf or two would go down before he died.

Nails on the hardwood floors had him looking at the doorway. When only Alexander was there and no Quinn, he asked how it had gone. The man looked wrecked.

"She's going up to change. I'm guessing that she means into a woman and not just her pants." Caleb told him more than likely. "I told her. She's a mite upset with me for not letting her know at the beginning, but I think she understands why I did it this way. I just wanted to spare her."

"She's a great deal stronger than you think. I'm sure that you meant well in keeping it from her. But from here on out, she'll be able to smell when you're sick afore you know it. And she'll be able to tell when you're keeping something from her." Alexander told Dad that he had her best interests at heart. "I can see that. I surely can. But hopefully Carmen can help you out. She's old. Pretty too."

They talked for a few minutes and Caleb realized that

Quinn was taking a long time. Getting up, he made his way to the stairs when he noticed the blood on the tile at the entrance hall. And the door was open.

Calling out her name, he took the stairs three at a time. When he saw the blood in the hall outside their bedroom, he felt his wolf run over his skin. He wanted out, to find his mate and to kill whoever took her. Going into the bedroom, he found her bathroom covered in blood, and more blood on the bed. He leaned to it and sniffed just as Dad and Alexander came into the room. Before he could tell them to stop, his dad did.

"Don't touch anything. I'm calling the boys now. We need a clean scent." Alexander asked what was going on. "He's been here, ain't he, son? He's gone and taken our Quinn."

"I think, yes. But all this blood isn't hers. However… Harley. He was in the office."

They all took off down the stairs at breakneck speed. Harley was just coming out of the office when he saw the blood. The screams that came from him made Caleb's wolf curl around him. The need to protect Harley was great. But he also knew that anyone here could take care of the young man; it was Quinn that he needed to find now.

"We'll get her back. I promise you. And when we find Wade, he is going to rue the day that he fucked with my family." Dad told him he'd help. "You can, by telling the rest of them that I've left to find her. And for them to come quickly."

"All right, but you be right careful, son. I don't want to have to tell your momma that you went and got hurt on account'a you being all macho. You know she won't be happy about that." He told him he'd be careful. "You just be safe. For all of us. And you bring that girl back home here. I've grown a mite fond of her, and I want her back too."

His wolf took him, not gently. It was harsh, painful, and his wolf was pissed off. As he made his way down the stairs, he paused by Harley. He was lying on the floor, his hands near the blood. He looked up at him and Caleb licked his face.

If he could have spoken to him, he would have told him he was getting her back. And when he did, someone was going to pay for this. As he left the house, he remembered the council and their request to lay low. Well fuck that shit, his mate was gone.

CHAPTER 12

Quinn wasn't sure at first where she was, but she knew that she wasn't home. Her head was hurting like someone had taken a bat to it, and she was sick to her stomach. Looking around the room, or wherever she was, she didn't move her body. There was no point in alerting anyone that she was awake if someone was watching her.

A light was burning about ten feet from her, but her head hurt too badly for her to make it out well. The room wasn't black dark, but it was too dark for her to make out anything around her. The thing that she was on was hard, so she thought maybe she was on the floor.

Where are you, love? She smiled. Of course, Caleb would have figured out she was missing. *I've been trying to be calm. Can you hear it in my voice? Mom told me if I upset you in any way, she was going to beat my bottom. I'm pretty sure she would too. I doubt very much she'd take in the fact that I'm a grown man with a mate, either.*

Your mom is scarily calm. I bet she said it in that soft southern voice of hers too. Caleb laughed and said that she had. *I don't know where I am. I just woke up. I had no idea he was even in the house.*

We didn't either. It wasn't until I came back that I was told that he was in the bedroom when you went up. His scent was all over our closet. She asked him where he'd gone. *I was determined that I was going to find you and bring you back. All I did was literally chase my tail for a few hours and grow a little more frustrated with each minute. My brothers took care to call in Daniel, and he had a team going over the house. They found where he'd been hiding, and smelled enough blood to know that you'd gotten in a few licks yourself. I should have asked you, are you hurt?*

I have a pounding headache, but it seems to be letting up a little. And I'm lying on a floor or something. It's hard and cold. He told her to see if she could smell anything. *Yeah, dirt. It stinks to high heaven here.*

What I mean is, as a wolf, you can separate some smells from others. Like I can smell fertilizer in the fresh tilled earth. The smell of roses at first bloom. You can as well. Just take in a deep breath and try to sort what you're familiar with from the things that you don't know. He paused for just a few seconds before continuing. *You can hear things too. Very well. Just close your eyes and let whatever is going on around you filter over you.*

She did as he asked, thinking at first he was being crazy. But then she started hearing things. Things she knew she wouldn't have heard as a human. Quinn started to think she could hear a fart in the next state over if she listened hard enough.

I hear cars. Not a lot of them, but a few. And trucks. They don't sound all that close, but I can hear them. He told her that was good, that meant that she wasn't near a highway. *I hear music. Not in here with me, but...I'm not sure. It sounds like canned music, like you'd hear on an elevator.*

What can you smell? What didn't she smell? But she tried to do as he'd told her, to take in a breath and figure it out. *There might be mold, or even trash. That'll be harder to sort. Also, you should be able to smell water if it's close.*

How does one smell water? He laughed and told her that she'd smell fish, or even sewage. *Gross. I'm sorry I asked. Okay, water. I don't know. Let me see.*

Closing her eyes again, she could hear things better now. The smells around her were there, stronger as well. The music was clearer; the bass was more pronounced. She realized then that it was moving toward her. Whatever was playing was moving.

The music is jazz, and it's closer than it was before. And getting closer all the.... The noise close to her startled her, and she knew that whatever had made it was in the room with her. *Wade is back. I haven't seen him yet, but I know that he's here.*

Okay, that helps. We've had pack on him for the last two hours. He came into town a bit after you were kidnapped...we think he was trying to establish an alibi. He was hurt too, so good for you.

Yeah, don't remember that much about it. But I do know that he was in the room with me, now that I think about it. I'm not sure he was waiting on me. He said something like I'd have to do, or something along those lines. I think he was looking for you. Caleb said he had his full attention now. *Are you going to kill him?*

Yes. The finality of the word scared her a little. Not that she didn't think the bastard needed to die, but Quinn knew that Caleb would show him no mercy. Much like Wade didn't to his latest victims. *We know where you are, love, and we're coming. Just hang on for me.*

The kick to her feet had her moaning, but she didn't speak. It wasn't until the light came on above her that she had a chance to look at the man. He looked like he'd gone a few rounds with...well, with her. She grinned when he put a tissue to his nose.

"You don't look so good there, Wade. What happened?

Did you bite off more than you could chew?" He kicked her again, this time in the ribs. "Why don't you let me go and I can show you what it's like when I'm not hit from behind?"

"You belong to me, bitch. And you taking a mate without my permission is going to get you both killed." She asked him if he thought that was the way things were going to go. "Oh, I know they will. As soon as he gets here, I'm going to teach him a lesson he won't soon forget. Then I'm going to take my time with you, showing you all the things that I should have done when I had you cornered like a frightened rabbit. If I remember correctly, you weren't even that tasty of a morsel either."

"What if I told you that Caleb is going to kill you? I mean, you're nothing but an old man, and he's young and vibrant. I think he can take care of you without even letting his wolf out." Wade laughed. "You think this is funny? I suppose I do too, now that you mention it."

"Yes, I do as a matter of fact. I'm an alpha and your mate is nothing more than a cog in the wheel of stupidity." She asked him what he meant by that. "He's nothing to me. The same as you. And once you are both dead, you'll know that no one mourned your death. No one cared that I took you out, and you can most certainly count on no one finding your body, even if it takes the next fifty years. I am going to take care that you're not even identifiable when I'm finished with you."

"You mean because you marked me for no other reason than you could, you're going to kill us? What kind of stupid shit are you pulling? Don't you care that someone might find a mate in your victims and they suffer for it?" He grinned at her while he confirmed it was his right. "Your right? How the fuck do you figure you had a right to bite me like you did?

Did you know because of what you did, I could have died?"

"So? Why would that matter to me? I mean, to have you dead then or now, it makes little difference to me. But this way, I get to kill myself a young pup who should have known better than to take what was already claimed." He sat in the chair that was sitting next to the table that she had noticed. "You don't seem to understand that as an alpha, one of my strength and age, there comes certain privileges that others, younger pups, cannot have yet. To have lived for so long and be what I am, it is a miracle that I've only killed the few that I have."

"So you admit to killing people for no other reason than that you wanted to." Wade shrugged. "You're a sick bastard. Did you know that?"

"It's an illusion I portray when I need to in order to get my way. Especially around wolf packs that I plan to take over soon." She asked him if it was Daniel's pack. "Of course. He knows that I'm in his territory, yet he has not once in all this time come to greet me. Offer his hand in friendship. I say that's very poor management on his part. Wouldn't you?"

"You're insane." He threw back his head in apparent mirth. "You kill because he didn't come and bow before you?"

"That would have been nice, but no. I would have done this regardless of his actions. It was just the icing on the cake, so to speak, that makes me want to do it more. And I'll tell you a bit of a secret. I really enjoy it too." Quinn felt Caleb in the room, and when Wade didn't turn, she thought he was ignoring Caleb to show off.

"And you marked me? Why did you do that?" He shrugged again. "You had to have a reason for it. I mean, what did you think was going to happen when you went around marking potential mates to other wolves?"

173

"Exactly what did happen. Women aren't worth all that much anyway. I mean, just look at you. Your mate, whoever he is, hasn't broken down my door to get you. I'm assuming that you've spoken to him. Told him all about this place. I even had the music that was playing in the bar next to us move themselves outside so that he could pinpoint you. But has he shown? No. And would you like to know why?" She didn't answer him, nor did she look in the direction she knew that Caleb was. "He didn't come because, like myself, he knew that he could get himself another bitch to spread her legs."

The low growl from the direction where Caleb was had Wade rising from his seat. He didn't look to her like a man who was the least bit frightened. When Caleb entered the room with two other men behind him, it took her several seconds to realize that it was his brother Gabe and Daniel. And Daniel looked like a man who was amused about something.

"Hello, Wade Douglas. I guess you've really fucked up this time." Wade slumped over, his body looked older in that second, like he was burdened with age. "What am I going to do with you? Oh, I remember. Nothing. Not a damned thing. I have no interest any longer in your actions nor your crimes. None."

Wade turned and winked at her, as if he knew that the man was going to say this to him. She struggled to sit up, thinking that if someone would just let her go, she'd do something to him, when Caleb sat at the head of the table, his brother to his right and Daniel the left. Caleb motioned for Wade to have a seat.

"Do you not care that I have your mate here, young Caleb?" Wade glanced at her, then sat at the table with the other men. "I told her that you'd feel this way about her. I'll tell you, I thought I was going to have to go through the act of

174

letting you think me old and feeble, but this is so much better. What is it you'd like to bargain with to get her back?"

"I'm not going to bargain at all. I'm going to ask you a few questions, and you'll either answer me or not. Right now, I could care less what you say." Wade leaned back in the chair, tilting it in a way that it was only on the back two legs. "Now, did you kidnap my mate by coming unannounced into my home to get her?"

"Of course I did. You can see her right here. I will say that she did put up a nice fight, but with my superior strength, I was able to take her out with one blow." Caleb didn't look at her, but she had a feeling that he was well aware of her. "Your next question?"

"The elderly lady in the parking garage, did you kill her for no other reason than she was in the way? Let me rephrase that. Did you—?"

"Yes, yes. I killed her. No matter how you say it, I did it. And if you want to know the truth of it, I rather enjoyed it too." Quinn wasn't sure what was going on, but was too afraid to ask. "You said a few questions, young pup. Are you about through, or are we going to be here all day while I wait for you to ask me about your mate? Come now, you do want her back, don't you?"

What if what Wade had told her was true? That no one would care if she was dead or not. Sitting up a little higher, she leaned her back against the wall and stared at the four men. What the hell was going on?

"There are three things you should know before we take care of this." Wade asked Caleb what that might be. "Well, Gabe here is now an enforcer. He's agreed to help out with the pack laws and rules, many of which you've broken today when you took my mate. The second thing is, Daniel has stepped down. He will attend to the sick."

"And you? What is it you've decided that I need to know? That you're pack alpha? I should hope that's what you're going to tell me. I think it will be a feeling like none other when I kill you."

Quinn would have missed the shift from man to beast had she not been looking right at Caleb. Not only did his shift take down the table, but it knocked Wade onto the floor. She watched as Caleb, as his wolf, put his paw on Wade's chest and his sharp claws raked down him.

The screams were loud. Wade begged for his life, pleaded with Caleb to let him go. But he only stood over him, his wolf staring down at the man he held with his paw. When she was touched on the arm, she looked at Daniel and he told her to come with him. Gabe cut the ropes that were around both her wrists and legs.

She hesitated when she was lifted up in Daniel's arms. He told her to hold on, that they were leaving. Quinn nodded once and he took her out of the room and on out into the sunshine. He was looking her over when she finally got up the nerve to ask him what was going to happen.

"To you? Nothing." He handed her a washcloth to clean her face. "I'd rather you not ask me about Wade. Caleb, he's going to take care of him with the help of Gabe. If he wants you to know what happens, then he'll tell you."

She asked him if it was true, that Caleb was the alpha now. He told her that he was, as she was as well. Then he moved away from her, close but not close enough for her to ask questions. The rest of Caleb's family showed up with her dad just as Gabe and Caleb came out of the building with Wade between them.

~~~

Carmen loved watching the young couple. She'd been friends with Caleb and his family for a long time. And it was good to see something wonderful coming to them finally. As she made her way toward Caleb and his new mate, she thought of all the things that she'd seen over her lifetime, and how much more she would enjoy the coming events now that the Winchester family was happy.

"I cannot thank you enough for your help." She told him it was her pleasure. "I wasn't sure it was going to work, to be honest."

"When I tell you that I can make you invisible to all, that is what I mean. Him not knowing you were alpha...well that was just some fun on my part. I hope you don't mind. And even if you did, I don't really care. I'm like that, you see." She turned to young Quinn. "You, however, startled me when you looked directly at Caleb. Did you see him or the three of them?"

"All of them. I wasn't sure why Wade hadn't. I thought that he was showing off at first, then when they came in.... Well, it matters little now. I know what you did, and I thank you as well." Carmen was impressed. This young woman was going to be fun to watch as she came into her own as an alpha bitch. "Will you be staying around? Caleb said that you don't live around here."

"No. I live far from here." When she didn't ask, Carmen smiled. "Thank you for that. A vampire never reveals where she lives nor who might be living with her. It's a safety thing, if you want to know the truth. Nor does she invite people to know unless she trusts them."

"I'd like to earn your trust, if you'd allow it. Enough that you'd come and stay with us when you're around. Or stay forever, I'd not mind. You saved us both today, I think."

Carmen told her that she was only a small bit of help. "If you say so, but I think had he gone in there with guns blazing, someone, if not all of us, would have been killed. I think you calmed him too. Didn't you?"

"Just a little. You're a very smart woman. Does Caleb appreciate you as much as he should?" Quinn lit up, her face bright with love, and it was a sight to behold. "I see that he does. Which is a good thing…it means that he knows what he has in you. And I would love to stay for a bit. If you're sure you don't mind."

"No. I think it would be wonderful." She flushed prettily. "I'm not positive what sort of accommodations you might need. We have a sub level that is completely furnished. You're welcome to that or anything we have when you're here."

"Thank you. The sub levels will be perfect." She liked this girl a great deal, and wanted to give her something special. "Would you take my hand?"

She gave it willingly, and Carmen smiled. There weren't any questions from her. Not any kind of hesitation. So, when their hands touched, then they held, Carmen passed onto the young woman a gift that would keep her and her family safe for all time.

They both turned when the howling started. Wade hadn't been killed. Yet. But when the council was finished with him, he most certainly would be. Carmen wondered if it would be Caleb that would get the pleasure, or the council would simply do it themselves. Either way, the man's days of terror were about to end.

"When Daniel lifted me up to take me out of the room, I thought for sure that Caleb was going to kill Wade. It's no less than he deserved, but I think something needed to be done first, like a trial of sorts." Carmen told her there would be one, and that it was going to start now. "Yes. Caleb told me when I asked him. I think...I know this sounds stupid, but I think that other people need to know his reasons for what he did. Not that they're justified, but so that others will know the consequences of actions like his."

"Wade is a very old wolf, I'm sure you're aware of that. And he's been getting away with his reign of terror for a very long time. No one, it seemed, wanted to deal with him. It's doubtful, had you and Caleb not taken over, he would have been brought to justice even now." Four men dressed in black were suddenly there. "That's the council. There are usually five, but they are a man short because of Wade. He killed the mate of the man that should be here, and he in turn killed himself."

"This isn't going to go well for him, is it? I know that I shouldn't care, but I hate to see anyone dead, even him." Wade was shoved to the ground; his neck was embraced in a silver chain. "Can you tell me what's going on?"

"Yes. They're reading his crimes to him. Not all, but the last several. The death of the woman in the garage. Also, as Caleb's mate, you're going to be mentioned as well. They will then read off the crimes that he committed to humans in general. These are the ones that the council will give the most punishment for. He let himself become a problem for their kind by allowing himself to be recorded." Quinn asked why the death of his kind wasn't more important. "It is. But with him becoming a problem with the humans, he has easily made it so that there are more hunters out looking for wolves. Of any kind."

"I see. So, he's in trouble for causing more deaths, not just the one with the woman and the others. You'd think he'd be making sure that all wolves are safe. But then he was biting

179

women in order not to let males find their mates."

They watched as the men read over the documents in their hands, each of them taking a turn to read. Caleb held the chain with gloves on. It was only a thin piece of silver, really, but it made it so that Wade couldn't shift and run. The tension between the men was great, and Carmen wondered how Caleb was holding onto his temper when each deed was read. Finally it was finished.

"Now that the list is read, he'll be given a chance to tell his side. I wouldn't want to be the one listening to that. I'm sure that he's going to say that he did it because he could." They both listened, and much to her surprise not only did he seem to think they had the wrong man, but he denied that he'd done a thing.

"Do they believe him? Surely they're not going to just let him go, are they? That would really piss me off."

Like Quinn, Carmen had little to no faith in this coming to a good end. Either they'd let him go with a warning or they'd put him in jail. A prison cell made of silver lining that he would spend the rest of his life in. Wade, in her opinion, needed to be dead. When he was jerked up from the ground, Carmen held her breath. It was over almost as soon as his feet were under him.

"They...they killed him." Carmen put out her hands to steady the young wolf. "They just took his head off. Just like that. I mean, I wanted him to be gone from our lives, and I knew that they'd kill him, but I never.... They removed his head."

"It was the only way to ensure that he was dead." Quinn nodded and said she was all right now. "You should know something more about the council. They'll make restitution to the dead. Not always in a monetary way, but in some way, they'll help all those that were affected by him."

"That's good. I mean…some of the people he hurt or killed, they're grieving deeply. I know that I was lucky in that I found Caleb and he was able to save me. But what of the others, the ones that have lost their lives?"

"Each of them will be helped." Quinn didn't ask more; she could have and Carmen would have told her that bills would suddenly be paid off. That a doctor who wasn't available before would be free to do a surgery or help with a baby. Christmas gifts would appear under the tree for the children left behind. The pack would help as much as they could, but the council would take care of the most of it.

Caleb came to join them then. Carmen watched as he held his bride. And when he looked at her, she could see his love for the woman in his arms. It made her feel great knowing that this man had found his one true love.

"I'm ready to meet your father now. If you don't mind, I'll meet you at the house." Caleb told her to come when she was ready. "I'll be there. And when I'm done, your lovely wife offered me a place to rest. Thank you both for that."

"Anytime, you know that."

She did too. As she made her way into the darkening night, she thought of the gift that she'd bestowed to Quinn. The gift of longer life was a power that she shared with very few. But she would the entire Winchester family.

181

CHAPTER 13

Caleb wanted to smack Alexander. He was having second thoughts on this. Carmen, as usual, was finding humor in the situation, and all he wanted to do was tell the older man to sit down, shut up, and do as he was told.

"Dad, why are you doing this?" Alexander looked at his daughter and opened his mouth, but she cut him off. "You don't want to see your grandchildren? Hold them and tell them stories as you did me? You should think about what you're going to miss. And how much we're going to miss you. Think of Harley."

"I do think of him, every day of my life. And of you. Seeing you so happy now, it's done me a world of good. But darling, I'm not well, and even if she could make me feel a little better, it won't keep me from getting worse."

"Oh, but it will." Caleb and the rest of them turned to Carmen. "I'm pretty sure that if you allow me to, I can make sure that your cancer is not just cured, but it won't ever affect you again. You'll be healthier than you have been for a long time." Alexander asked if she was going to change him into a vamp. "No, but if you'd like I can do that as well. It might be fun for me to take you to my bed once you're strong enough to take me."

"Now see here. I'm a married man." Carmen laughed and so did Caleb. There wasn't ever a time when this woman had a filter where her mouth was. "You're just funning me. I see how you are. But this cancer, it's eaten me up. I have it on my brain too."

"I know just where it is, Alexander. You have it in your blood, as well as your bone marrow. I can help you." Carmen put out her hand. "If you wish, I can help you to live a long and happy life with your daughter and her family. Or I can hasten your death so that you won't suffer. And you will, you know that."

"They told me that I'd be a monster before this was done. Not those words, but close enough." Carmen nodded. "What is it you're going to do to me? Exactly. I don't want any surprises."

"I'll bite you. Then when I've taken as much of your blood as I can, I'll give you mine. I will make you rest during this. It can be quite painful, and your body will.... It will need time to rest after the cancer is gone. After a few days, you'll wake and you'll be as well as you've ever been before this." Alexander asked if he would feel it. "No. I'll make sure that you don't feel anything other than the taste I will take of you to put you to rest."

"I don't mean to be rude or anything, but I'm a businessman first and foremost. What is this gonna cost me? Or whoever you're doing this for?" She looked at Caleb and he nodded once. Alexander huffed at him. "You aren't paying her for this for me. If anyone does, it'll be myself. I'm the sick one."

"No one is paying me, Alexander. And though it was offered, I cannot take it. Twenty years ago, I was found out by a group of men that meant to.... Well, let's just say that they decided that I was theirs to play with as they wanted. They had tied me to the barn with silver and were commencing to have their way with me. Until a young man, still in school, came to my rescue. Not only did he make sure they saw the error of their ways, but I believe he might have hurt them in ways that they'd remember for a very long time. Then he set me free." Everyone turned to look at Caleb as Carmen continued her story. "He cut me down then attended to my wounds. Then he did the most incredibly unselfish thing that anyone has ever done for me. He gave me a bit of his blood to save my life."

"You're making me out to be a hero, and all I did was be a prince to your damsel in distress. I think that's what you said to me when you were well enough to speak." She said it was. And she'd never forgotten it. "Me either. You've more than repaid me. You've been a very good friend."

"Thank you. But so have you." Carmen looked at Alexander. "You will allow me to do this for you, to pay on the debt of my life that I owe this man." Alexander said he would. "Thank you, my friend. You will not regret this."

Caleb held his hand. The grip that the man had on it was strong, but he knew when the bite was having its effect on him. Soon, his hand lay limply in his own palm and Caleb asked what he could do to help now.

"Nothing. I have it under control. I think, for the time being, you should take your lovely wife into the yard beyond and have a nice romp in the forest. We'll be just fine here, the two of us." He looked at Quinn, who he knew wanted to stay. *Take her, Caleb. There is no reason for her to be here when I do this. It will frighten her more to see it.*

He finally convinced Quinn to leave with him. They were in the yard when he realized that Carmen was right. There wasn't any reason for her to watch the process. While it was simple, he knew that when Alexander *rested*, he would be near death.

"Here is what we're going to do. You're going to shift then take off to the woods. And once you're there, I want you to try and hide from me. I'm going to find you then fuck you hard." She took a step back from him, not from fear but in excitement. "Go, now, before I change my mind and take you right here."

She let her wolf take her. Caleb thought that he was prepared for her beauty. The white wolf was startling against the green of the grass. When she took off to the woods, he watched her, knowing that she was the most beautiful creature he'd ever seen, or would ever see again. Just as he was ready to shift himself, Carmen spoke to him.

I've given her long life. He paused in pulling his shirt off. *When you make love to her, you too will live a long time as well. I plan to give the same gift to your family. There is no reason for you to die when I can keep you around for my entertainment.*

I'm not sure what to say. She told him to say thank you. *Yes, thank you very much. But this is something.... Thank you. I'm sure that my family will as well.*

He let his wolf take him. As soon as he was down on all fours, he felt the difference in his body. Caleb was larger, his muscle mass thicker. He had expected some magic to come to him when he agreed to take the pack, but he thought it would be slower in coming. As he made his way to the tree line, he thought of some of the other things that Daniel had told him about.

"You have about seventy in your pack. Most of them are older, set in their ways, but for the most part, no issues. I'm hoping that with you being in charge, younger wolves will come to us, or even come back. The lure of the bigger cities with larger packs is hurting the smaller ones. But, you should know that it's a very profitable pack." Caleb asked him what he meant. "There is enough money in the coffers for you to make any improvements needed, food in the pantry for a long while, as well as I'm staying on as a doctor for you."

He saw Quinn as soon as he entered the darkened woods. She'd have to work on being careful when she was hiding in the future. With her white fur, she stood out brightly in any situation. Carefully, he made his way to her, watching her as he went.

This is a lot more difficult than I thought it would be. He asked her why. *Well, I keep getting distracted by every little sound and color. I can see things a lot clearer than I do when I'm a human. Or it could be because I'm more aware of them.*

It's more than likely both. You're beautiful. Have I said that to you today? She laughed and said that he had. *Well, it bears repeating.*

He moved to stand next to her, rubbing his larger body to hers. As he was nipping her on the back, she moved away to stand next to the creek that ran lazily down the back of their property.

I know that we talked about children, but I was wondering how many you might want. We talked about hundreds, but I'm sure you don't want that many. I mean, I'm assuming that you want a few, coming from a large family. I do too. He sat down, waiting for her to get to the reason she'd brought it up now. *Do you know that there are three children in your pack who have no one to claim them? Alisha, Daniel's wife, told me about them.*

There was a car accident a few months ago. I knew that the pack was caring for them, but I never thought of them beyond that. What do you want to do, Quinn? Adopt them? I wouldn't mind that. He watched her pace, her beautiful animal making no sound as

187

she did so. *If you would like we can do it now. But someday, I'd really like to see you round with our child.*

I want a child of yours. Very much so. He nipped her again, this time a little harder. *Why does that make me wet?*

Christ, woman. The things that spill from your mouth at times. He moved to stand over her, his wolf wanting his mate. *I want you. Right now.*

Good. Because I don't think I can wait much longer. He explained to her about sex between them, how his wolf would dominate her and she'd just have to take it. *I read about it. Your mom kindly gave me a guide book. It's very strange that she felt I'd need to know this part, don't you think?*

He didn't care, so long as she was his. As he mounted her, pushing her head to the ground, her wolf growled and fought him. Instead of making his wolf pissy that she wasn't taking it, he seemed to enjoy her fighting. And when he finished, giving her a part of his body that would mark her for all males, he leaned back on his haunches and howled.

Caleb looked at his mate. She was human again, her nude body glistening in the afternoon sun. She looked good enough to eat, and his wolf moved forward as if he'd been given permission to do just that.

"Please, Caleb, I need you."

His wolf lapped at her from gate to clit. The scream that came from her made birds fly from the trees above them, the crickets and other animals scurry to get away. The second time he made her come, his wolf growled low in his throat and brought her again.

You're delicious. Like nothing I've ever tasted before. Her head nodded, her body trembled. *Come for us, Quinn, then I'll take you.*

She cried out again, her body bowing up off the ground

as she did so. His wolf let him go then, and instead of moving up her body as he wanted, he buried his face over her, taking her clit into his mouth and nipping gently at her tender flesh.

"No more. Please, no more." He took his time moving up her body, tasting little bits of her as he went. A taste of her hip, the flesh below her navel. Her ribs were next, licking a path up to her breast. "Caleb, take me."

"I am. But my way." He suckled at both her nipples. Caleb moved to her throat, careful not to bite her yet but tasting the dewiness of her skin. When he took her lobe into his mouth, he slid his cock into her heat and took her slowly as he moved his mouth to hers. "Kiss me, Quinn. I want to make love to my dear wife."

Caleb took her slowly, marveling at the way her body accepted his, how she fit beneath him. He loved her. Loved her with all his heart and soul. She was the very reason, he knew, that he'd been born. And when he released with her, their bodies becoming one, he held her in his arms like she was the most precious thing in the world. And to him, she was.

~~~

Sara sat on the swing she'd gotten several years ago for a birthday present. It was her time, just before dinner and the preparation of fixing it. As she moved back and forth, she thought of the young woman that had come to be with Caleb, how much happier he seemed and much more relaxed. When the swing moved suddenly, she looked at the intruder and smiled at her mate.

"You okay with me joining you for a spell? I got me a powerful need to just hold your hand for a bit." She put her hand out and he took it in his, kissing the back of it as he sat. "I'm so in love with you, Sara dear, I can hardly believe my

189

luck."

"I love you too, even though there are times when I want to strangle you a bit. But I was thinking of Caleb and Quinn. They're so happy together." He agreed as he set the swing into motion. Sara didn't care to swing, not like her husband did. She just moved back and forth; he acted as if he were trying to go someplace. "We're having Thanksgiving at their home, did I tell you that? Of course, it'll not be the same without having everyone here, but I'm excited to pass on this tradition."

"So long as you make me a graham cracker applesauce cake, I don't care where we have it. And your famous pie. You know how much I like your sweet potato pie." She did. He would try to take pieces of it almost as soon as it came out of the oven. "Why did you let them take it if'n you're gonna miss it so much?"

"I wasn't asked. I just told them that since they had that big house, they should host it. I think it'll be a nice change for me, don't you? Not to have to spend all my time in the kitchen while you get to visit." He nodded and smiled. "Do slow down, Kelley. What if we have a new grandbaby here with us? You'd surely hurt it with the way you're going at it."

He stopped swinging and nearly tossed her out of the infernal thing. He looked so shocked that she looked around to see what had upset him. When he started swinging again, it was sedate and almost too slow.

"A grandbaby. Never thought about it, to be honest. Oh my, oh my, a little one in the house again. Might be the best thing ever about having kids if you can have yourself a grandbaby." She agreed, but pointed out that the boys were very nice too. "They are. Surely they are. But I'd like to see me a granddaughter or two. A little girl that will look up to me like I'm special only to her. And piggy tails in her hair.

Wouldn't that be a hoot?"

"You're very special to me too, you old turd." He laughed like she wanted him to. "Caleb and Quinn having a baby will be wonderful, don't you think? I mean, I know they've only been together for a little while, but I think it would be so nice to have a baby by next Christmas. We'll spoil it rotten, too."

"Durn tootin' we will. I'm thinking we should start on that spoiling thing now." She asked him how that was going to come about. "I think a nice swing set would be about the right thing. Put up one of them fancy ones that we seen in a catalog. You know the one."

"Yes, the wooden kind." He said that was it. "What will the boys think? Us putting up a swing set without any children in the household? They might have us put away in some nursing home, thinking that we're addled for something."

"Don't care. I'm gonna go ahead and order it. Mayhap it'll inspire them to help us have a reason for putting it in. We'd have to have it put together by somebody. I don't have it in me anymore to do it myself. Besides, you know me and instructions." She did. He didn't like to have someone telling him how to put things together. She usually had to make him. But the idea of the swing set was starting to warm her a bit. "And if'n they don't have us grandkids, we'll just have it for the pack kids. With Caleb being the alpha now, they'll be around a bit more."

"I could crochet. I've not done it for years. Booties. I'm going to get some yarn and do booties." She looked over at her husband, who was struggling to find a number for the swing set when she took his new phone from him and found it. Handing it back, she continued. "Oh Kelley, we're going to be grandparents, I just know it."

They were loading up in the car to go to the store for yarn

191

and things when Caleb and Quinn came by. Kelley said they'd not tell him just yet, and she agreed. Hugging them both, they sat back on the porch to talk. Her son looked as if he were going to burst with good news.

"Quinn and I have talked it over, and we're going to adopt the Sawyer children." Sara felt her heart skip several beats. This was wonderful news, but she waited for the rest. "We're going to have children of our own too, but we feel that with this added windfall that we've been given, that we can help out—"

"Woo hoo, I'm gonna be a grandda! When? You gonna go and get them today? Your momma and I, we've been planning for this, yes sir we have. Gonna have a swing set put in." Kelley hugged Caleb, then Quinn, twice before he sat back down, nearly unseating her in his exuberance with the swing. "We're going to be the best grandparents ever. And your daddy? He must be about to bust a gut. I am."

"I can tell. And we've not told him. He's...I guess he's resting." Sara had forgotten about that, that poor Alexander was getting taken care of. "Caleb talked to Carmen and she told him that he's doing well now. We are hoping for the best."

"As you should. Yes, that's a good thing she's doing for this family." Kelley looked over at her. "We should plan a dinner. A big family dinner for when he wakes up."

"Oh, yes, that's a great idea. I'll set it all up, and we'll have it two weeks from today. That should give him plenty of time to be better and me to get it organized." Quinn said she'd help any way she could. "I would love that. My newest daughter in my kitchen with me. We'll have so much fun."

As soon as the couple left them, her and Kelley got into their car and made their way to town. They had a mission now, food and planning. Yarn and the lumber store. There would be presents too, for the little ones. Sara thought they were young, none of the children above nine or ten.

"Those kids that they're taking, what do you know about them? I know their parents were killed recently, but I don't remember how." She told him about the car accident that took both their lives. "Oh, I remember now. They were going to dinner and some drunk hiney wipe slammed into their car. Poor mites. They'll do well to have Caleb and Quinn as parents. Won't take the place of their own, but they'll be loved and cared for."

"Yes, and have a large extended family as well. The oldest, I think, is about eight. The youngest might be two, but I don't remember." Kelley told her that sounded about right, and the middle one was five. "And with Christmas only a few months away, we'll have to hurry and get them all nice gifts. Fun things. I'm not going to be that grandma that buys them clothing. Toys. We'll outfit them in toys."

"I'm gonna get them fishing poles." She stared at her husband. As far as she knew he'd never even baited a hook before. "I can learn it. Ain't nothing to it but drop a hook in the water, right?"

"I have no idea. But I think you might have time to figure it out. Also, equipment. I'm sure that it takes specialized equipment to go fishing." She had an idea that he'd have every gadget there was before summer came around again. Her excitement overwhelmed her. "Oh, Kelley, we're going to be grandparents. I'm so excited I could just cry about it. And so soon too. Do you think now that Caleb has a mate, the other boys will too soon?"

"Don't be crying, love. You know how that hurts me. Even with it being good tears, it just about rips my heart out. But I don't see any reason they should be left out of having a mate. They might not be as fun as Quinn, but they'll be loved, that's for tooting sure." She loved this man, and when he took her hand into his, she held it tightly. "I'm right proud of our boys. We did good, raising them up to be men of worth. Don't you think?"

"Yes. They had a good upbringing. The best we could have given them." She closed her eyes, thinking of the little babies she'd given birth to who were now grown men. "Kelley, do you suppose that one of them will have us a granddaughter? I know that the Sawyer children are all boys, but it would be nice to have a little girl to play with."

"You betcha. I'm betting we have all the granddaughters we will ever want." She would love them either way, but a granddaughter was something that she needed. "Don't know much about little girls and all, but I'm thinking that any our boys have won't be girly. Might be, but I don't know, really."

"I should hope one of them is. I'd hate to have to see a little one of theirs dressed in jeans and a T-shirt. I want frills and curls. Pink and dollies. Oh, Kelley, I need a little girl to dress up." He laughed and she smiled. "I guess that was a little over the top. But I would love to see just one before I turn up my toes."

They ended up shopping much longer than she'd thought. Her cart had been nearly overflowing with different colors of yarn and new needles. Having ready money wasn't something she was used to, and found that she could enjoy having it around for special things like this. As they made their way to their car again, their arms overloaded with bags, she thought about the children coming to them, how exciting it was going to be.

"How about I take my darling wife to dinner?" She nodded, loving this man more and more with each passing minute. "We can go to that nice steak house on the other side of town. I'm in the mood for somebody just waiting on us. And then taking the dishes away to clean up for you."

"Caleb Kelley Winchester. You are waited on every night, and the kitchen is cleaned up afterwards. What a thing to say." Before she could let her temper become full blown, he handed her a rose. A single pink rose. "You old turd, you."

"I love you. So much sometimes I just love seeing you get your dander up so I can surprise you a bit." He kissed her and Sara felt tears fill her eyes. "All my life, even before I met you, I knew there would be one special woman out there for me. Little did I know that she'd come along and make me not just love her, but worship her. Sara Winchester, you are my heart and my soul, and I just don't know what I'd do without you."

Before You Go...

HELP AN AUTHOR

write a review

THANK YOU!

Share your voice and help guide other readers to these wonderful books. Even if it's only a line or two your reviews help readers discover the author's books so they can continue creating stories that you'll love. Login to your favorite retailer and leave a review. Thank you.

AWARD WINNING, BESTSELLING AUTHOR

Kathi Barton, winner of the Pinnacle Book Achievement award as well as a best-selling author on Amazon and All Romance books, lives in Nashport, Ohio with her husband Paul. When not creating new worlds and romance, Kathi and her husband enjoy camping and going to auctions. She can also be seen at county fairs with her husband who is an artist and potter.

Her muse, a cross between Jimmy Stewart and Hugh Jackman, brings her stories to life for her readers in a way that has them coming back time and again for more. Her favorite genre is paranormal romance with a great deal of spice. You can visit Kathi online and drop her an email if you'd like. She loves hearing from her fans. aaronskiss@gmail.com.

Follow Kathi on her blog: http://kathisbartonauthor. blogspot.com/

www.ingramcontent.com/pod-product-compliance
Lightning Source LLC
Chambersburg PA
CBHW032133170626
46808CB00006B/2220